I0642692

LOVE IS A LOADED CLIP

A Romantic Thriller Novel

by
Jahari Hasahi Malik

Ember Root Publishing
Fresno, California

First Edition – September 2025

`</div>`

Jahari Hasahi Malik

For permissions, licensing, or other inquiries, please contact:
Ember Root Publishing
[info@emberrootspublishing.com]
ISBN (Paperback): 979-8-9997450-4-9
ISBN (eBook): 979-8-9997450-5-6
First Edition: September 2025
Cover Design: Ember Root Creative Studio
Editor: Wendell J. King]
Printed in the United States of America

Jahari Hasahi Malik

Prologue

Some nights don't end. They burn.

The city groaned beneath a storm of sirens and smog, its arteries clogged with secrets and sin. High above it all, on the edge of a rooftop bathed in low orange light, I watched the skyline breathe like it was trying to forget what it saw.

The gun in my hand was still warm.

Blood was drying under my nails—some his, some mine, maybe some from the version of myself I wouldn't get back.

"Colt," Nay said behind me. Voice low, bruised from screaming. "You ready to tell me the truth now?"

I didn't turn around. Not yet.

Not while the heat from the last shot still lingered in the air like a kiss you regret.

Truth?

The truth was, I'd never meant to love her.

Not in a life like this.

Not with enemies who smiled in your face and pulled triggers behind your back.

Not when every time I touched her, it felt like lighting a fuse to a bomb I built myself.

But here we were.

Me with nothing left but vengeance and a promise.

Her with a body that healed like fire and eyes that begged me to stop lying to both of us.

Love doesn't save you in our world.

It *loads the clip*.

Love is a Loaded Clip

And when it's time to shoot, you don't hesitate.

Chapter 1 – The Cost of Clean Hands

Rain bled from the sky in streaks of neon and shadow, the kind of night where the city felt alive enough to bite.

The wet asphalt reflected red and gold from corner liquor stores and flickering streetlamps, and I could feel its hunger in my bones.

The streets had a rhythm, and I moved with it—hood up, hands buried in my jacket, pulse sharp.

My sneakers slapped against puddles, and for a second, the sound almost swallowed the low hum of a car rolling too slow down the block.

Trouble, my instincts whispered.

I ducked into the alley, narrow and slick with yesterday's trash, heart thudding. I wasn't scared, not exactly—I'd lived in these streets long enough to know fear didn't save you. But something electric coiled in my chest.

That's when I saw him.

Leaning against a graffiti-stained wall like he owned it, a cigarette glowing between his fingers. Hood half-down, sharp jaw, eyes like the last warning before a storm. His presence wasn't just physical—it was magnetic, dangerous.

"You lost?" His voice was smooth steel.

"No." I didn't blink. "City's mine same as yours."

He smirked, slow, deliberate, letting the cigarette dangle from his lips. "Then you know you just stepped into a dead zone."

Love is a Loaded Clip

The car that had been tailing me rolled past the mouth of the alley. Blacked-out windows. Music so low I could feel the bass more than hear it. My gut twisted.

"Who's after you?" he asked, like he already knew.

"Who says anyone is?"

He flicked the cigarette into the puddle. Steam hissed up like the city exhaled. Then he closed the distance, slow and predatory, his body heat searing in the cold night air.

"You smell like trouble," he murmured. "And I like trouble."

A shout cracked the night. Tires screeched.

Instinct moved us both—he grabbed my wrist and yanked me behind the dumpster just as gunfire split the rain. Sparks burst from metal and brick, and my heart kicked into overdrive.

He pushed me against the wall, shielding me with his body, heat and danger wrapped tight in leather and adrenaline. The city felt alive in that moment, pulsing through us.

"You bring this storm with you?" I whispered.

He glanced toward the street, then back at me, a grin curling like sin. "Baby, I *am* the storm."

We ran together after that—out of the alley, across the streaming streets, hearts colliding with every step. I didn't know his name yet, but I knew he wasn't leaving my story.

And I didn't know if that would save me or kill me.

Rain hit harder now, bouncing off the streets in silver sprays. My hoodie clung to me, soaked through, every step splashing the rhythm of escape. The stranger ran beside me, silent except for his controlled breaths and the steady thud of his boots.

We cut down another alley, then a narrow side street that smelled of wet concrete and fried food from a 24-hour spot. Somewhere far off, sirens wailed, but they weren't for us—yet.

"Who the hell are you?" I demanded, spinning to face him. My pulse hadn't calmed; it pulsed in my throat.

"Colt," he said simply, like that was enough. Rain ran down his jawline, his dark eyes catching stray light. "And you?"

A second stretched too long between us. I should've lied, but adrenaline doesn't care about strategy.

"Nay."

The name settled in the air between us like smoke. He nodded, taking me in like he was memorizing the edges of my face for later.

"You always make a habit of drawing fire?"

"You always make a habit of catching strays?"

His mouth curved, a grin sharp enough to cut.

A door slammed somewhere behind us.

Colt grabbed my hand without asking, and heat shot up my arm despite the cold rain. He pulled me into the shadow of a stairwell as a black SUV cruised past, its tires hissing against the street.

Through the rain-blurred glass, I saw a face—bald, with a scar running along the cheek. The man's gaze swept the street like he could smell me hiding.

The SUV rolled on.

Colt didn't let go of my hand right away. His thumb dragged once along my knuckles, deliberate, before he finally released me.

"You got someone hunting you," he said, voice lower now, more dangerous. "And I need to know why before I decide if I'm saving you or selling you."

The words hit, but instead of fear, a strange heat coiled in my chest. He wasn't bluffing, and maybe that's what made him more dangerous than the bullets.

"You planning to save me tonight?" I asked.

His grin widened just a fraction. "I already did."

Another distant pop of gunfire cracked the air, muffled by the rain. Neither of us flinched this time.

We moved again, fast and quiet, until the city swallowed us into a district of shuttered storefronts and flickering lights. Colt pushed open a side door to a building that looked abandoned, metal hinges squealing in protest.

Inside was warmth, low light, the faint hum of life somewhere above. The room smelled like leather, cigarettes, and faint gun oil.

He closed the door behind me. Rainwater dripped from our clothes to the dusty floor, echoing in the quiet.

"You shouldn't be out here alone," he said.

"I've been alone my whole life," I shot back, leaning against the wall, refusing to let him see my knees tremble.

"That's the problem," he murmured, stepping closer.

He didn't touch me. Not yet. But the way his eyes held mine was hotter than hands could be. I couldn't tell if I wanted to run or close the distance. Maybe both.

Outside, the city howled like it knew we had just set something dangerous in motion.

The building hummed with a low, electrical buzz. Somewhere upstairs, footsteps creaked, and a door slammed shut.

Colt didn't look concerned, which only made me more aware of how much he owned whatever space he walked into.

"You live here?" I asked, wringing rainwater from my hoodie sleeve.

"Sometimes." He shrugged, moving deeper into the room. "Depends on the night, depends on the heat."

"Heat like gunfire?"

He shot me a sharp glance, and for a second, the air between us went razor-thin.

"Heat like trouble," he said finally, voice a lazy drawl that made me wonder which kind of trouble he preferred.

I followed him past a row of cracked windows, the city lights bleeding through in crooked streaks.

Love is a Loaded Clip

The room opened into what had to be a repurposed loft: a worn leather couch, a table scattered with playing cards and bullet casings, and a duffel bag that sagged with the weight of secrets.

Colt dropped onto the couch, leaning back like a king on a throne of shadows. His eyes tracked me as I moved closer, each step deliberate, though my heart kicked like it wanted out of my chest.

"You're good at running," he said.

"I'm better at surviving."

He smirked. "We'll see."

I didn't know why I let him draw me in. Maybe it was the city in his voice, all grit and danger, or the way he occupied the room like he'd written his name in the walls.

Maybe it was because, for the first time in a long time, someone looked at me like I was more than a shadow slipping through streets.

"You gonna tell me who's after you?" he asked.

My lips parted, but no sound came out. The truth was heavy, a weight I hadn't shared with anyone.

"It's complicated."

"That's my favorite kind."

I drifted closer, and he didn't move—just watched, unblinking, like a predator testing my nerve. The city outside hissed with passing cars and rain, but here, the air thickened.

I stopped when I was close enough to feel the heat radiating off his skin. He smelled like rain, smoke, and adrenaline. Dangerous. Alive.

"Careful," he said softly, his gaze dropping briefly to my mouth. "You don't know what happens when you step too close."

"Maybe I'm tired of staying far away."

His hand lifted, slow enough to give me time to stop him, but I didn't. His fingers brushed my jaw, tracing a line that sent sparks racing down my spine.

He tilted my chin up slightly, holding me with the same certainty he had back in the alley when bullets kissed the rain.

"You've got fire in you," he murmured.

"Or maybe I'm just tired of running."

The distance between us dissolved. My pulse roared, but I didn't flinch. This wasn't love. It wasn't safety. It was a collision waiting to happen, and the city seemed to know it, breathing in through the cracked windows, whispering promises and warnings.

Then, a sharp noise shattered the moment— metal clanging against metal from somewhere below.

Colt's head snapped toward the sound, his entire body tensing in an instant. He was on his feet, a gun in hand I hadn't even seen him reach for.

"Stay here," he ordered, voice like steel.

But my feet moved anyway, following him to the edge of the stairs, every nerve in my body alive. The city hadn't finished with us yet.

The stairwell reeked of rust and old water. Each step down groaned beneath our weight, broadcasting us to whoever—or whatever—was in the shadows below. Colt's gun led the way, his movements silent and surgical.

A faint scraping echoed from the alley entrance.

He froze, arm stretched slightly to stop me from moving forward. My back pressed against the wall, heart pounding so loud I swore whoever was down there could hear it.

The door at the bottom swung open with a slow, complaining creak. A figure stepped into the faint spill of streetlight—hood pulled low, sneakers soaked, hands empty but tense.

"Don't," Colt said, his voice carrying the weight of a promise and a threat.

The hooded figure hesitated.

"I'm not here to fight," he said, voice hoarse from either running or fear. "But you need to know—they're coming. Tonight."

My throat went dry.

"Who's 'they'?" I asked, and my voice trembled despite me.

The hood dropped slightly, and I recognized the face. Darren. A name I hadn't said out loud in months. A name I thought I'd buried along with the mess he dragged me into.

"You shouldn't have shown your face here," I hissed, instinct pushing me a step back.

Darren's eyes flicked to Colt, calculating, then back to me.

"They're already looking for you. Scar's crew. They're saying you owe blood for what went down at the docks. If you stay here—"

The sentence never finished.

Jahari Hasahi Malik

Glass shattered somewhere above us.

Colt moved before thought, shoving me hard against the wall just as a round of gunfire ripped through the stairwell. Bullets sparked against metal, the echo a violent roar in the small space.

Darren dove down the last few steps, covering his head.

"Upstairs!" Colt barked, hauling me back toward the loft without waiting for agreement. His grip was firm, unshakable, a lifeline in chaos.

We reached the main room, adrenaline burning through the air like smoke. Colt shoved a table against the door in one sharp motion, then spun to face me, chest heaving.

"You weren't lying," he said.

I couldn't even answer. My lungs felt like they were filled with ice, my pulse trying to outrun the city itself.

He closed the distance in two strides, catching my face in his hand, eyes boring into mine.

"You got me into a war tonight, Nay."

"I didn't—"

"Doesn't matter," he cut in, low and rough. "You're in it now."

His mouth found mine before I could think, a hard, claiming kiss that tasted like rain, danger, and everything I'd been running from.

My body betrayed me, heat flooding through every nerve as I grabbed the front of his shirt like it was the only thing keeping me upright.

For one reckless heartbeat, the world outside disappeared. No bullets, no debt, no fear. Just him—sharp, hot, and alive.

Then the pounding started on the downstairs door.

Scar's crew had arrived.

Colt broke the kiss, resting his forehead against mine for a single electric second.

"Stay behind me," he said, voice like fire in the dark.

Outside, the storm had only just begun.

Chapter 2 Colt's Code –

The pounding at the door rattled the floorboards, and I could almost feel each hit in my ribs. Colt didn't flinch. He moved toward the window, scanning the alley below like he was calculating a chessboard no one else could see.

"They'll come up the back stairwell too," he said, voice steady. "They always do."

I hugged myself, soaked clothes clinging like a second skin, every nerve vibrating with adrenaline.

"What now?"

He glanced at me, eyes dark with more than just calculation.

"Now, we move. But first—" His gaze flicked to the blood running from a shallow cut across my thigh, exposed where my wet shorts clung to me. "You're hurt."

Before I could respond, he was crouched in front of me, fingers brushing carefully over my skin. The touch was electric.

"It's just a scratch," I whispered, trying to convince both of us.

"Even a scratch can get you killed if you're bleeding in the wrong street," he murmured, and there was something protective in the way he said it that made my chest tighten.

When his thumb swept the edge of the cut, heat flared low in my stomach. I wanted to move, to step back—but I didn't.

"You're shaking," he said.

"Because they're trying to kill me," I said, but it came out softer than I meant, my voice catching on the charge between us.

Colt rose slowly, so close that my breath hitched. His hand came up, knuckles brushing along my jaw like he was testing if I'd pull away.

I didn't.

The kiss that followed was slower than the first, deeper, like he wanted to memorize the shape of my mouth. His tongue teased mine, and my fingers curled in his shirt, pulling him closer until his body pressed firmly against mine, pinning me lightly against the cold wall.

Heat bloomed through me, pulse thrumming in my ears louder than the shouts echoing from below. His hands traced my hips, careful but hungry, sliding beneath the wet hem of my hoodie.

"You're trouble," he breathed against my lips.

"You kissed me first," I whispered, shivering with a mix of desire and danger.

A bang from downstairs snapped the spell.

Colt stepped back, jaw tight, gun already in his hand like it had never left.

"Time to move." He grabbed the duffel bag from the couch and slung it over his shoulder. "Stay on my heels. Don't stop for anything."

I nodded, breath still ragged from more than just fear, as we slipped into the narrow back hallway that smelled of dust and old rain.

We crept down a side stairwell, the sound of our pursuers now mixed with distant sirens. The city pulsed around us, alive with danger and temptation, like it knew we had crossed a line we could never return from.

The back stairwell opened to an alley glistening with rain, the puddles reflecting fractured neon signs from the street above.

The air smelled of gasoline and wet concrete, the kind of night the city used to wash itself clean of sins it never stopped committing.

Colt slipped into the shadows first, silent as a ghost, then crooked a finger for me to follow. My sneakers splashed lightly in the puddles as I hugged the wall.

We moved fast, weaving between dumpsters and fire escapes. My heart was hammering from the run and from the way his hand brushed mine every time he guided me around a corner.

"Stop." His voice was a whisper, sharp and commanding.

We froze in the dark gap between two shuttered storefronts. A black SUV rolled slowly down the block, headlights cutting through the mist. Scar's crew.

Colt pressed me back against the brick wall and flattened himself in front of me, shielding me with his body. His warmth seeped through my wet clothes, and even in danger, the nearness of him made my stomach tighten.

The SUV paused, its engine growling low.

I held my breath, cheek brushing the damp brick, his chest firm against mine. His hand found my hip, steadying me, thumb drawing an absentminded circle that sent a shiver down my spine.

"You're shaking again," he whispered, lips brushing the shell of my ear.

"I'm freezing," I said, but the heat pooling in me betrayed the lie.

His mouth lingered there a second longer than necessary, the softest graze of teeth against skin. My pulse jumped.

The SUV rolled forward.

Colt didn't move yet. He stayed close, his gaze locked on the street while his body held me against the wall like I was his to guard—or claim.

"I can hear your heart," he murmured, voice low enough to make it feel like a secret.

I swallowed hard. "Then you know exactly what you're doing to me."

A smirk ghosted across his face, but it vanished when a second set of headlights turned onto the street.

"Move," he said.

We sprinted across the alley, ducking through a chain-link fence with a panel cut out near the bottom. Colt went first, then reached back for me, pulling me through with strong, rough hands. The contact lingered a beat too long.

We hit another side street, deserted except for flickering streetlights and the distant hum of traffic. Colt led us into a recessed doorway of an abandoned building, pulling the duffel tight against his shoulder.

Inside, it smelled like mildew and old iron. Rain dripped through holes in the ceiling, each drop echoing in the empty space.

"Temporary stop," he said, scanning the shadows. "We wait for them to pass. Then we move."

I leaned against a pillar, adrenaline still spiking. My hands trembled, and Colt noticed. He set the duffel down and closed the distance between us in two long steps.

"You need to warm up," he said, voice low, almost rough.

Before I could respond, he shrugged out of his soaked jacket and wrapped it around my shoulders. His hands lingered on my arms, sliding down, fingers brushing against the thin line of skin where my hoodie had ridden up.

The world outside felt like it had fallen away, leaving just us and the sound of rain dripping in the dark.

"I shouldn't want you right now," I whispered, half-ashamed, half-daring him.

"But you do," he said, his eyes catching the sliver of light from the street. "And I do too."

His hand tipped my chin up, and he kissed me again—slower, deeper, as if the danger outside demanded we claim something inside. My fingers tangled in his shirt, pulling him down against me, and for a moment, the thrill of survival and raw desire blurred into one pulse.

The rain outside had slowed to a drizzle, but the city hadn't gone quiet—tires hissed over wet asphalt, and somewhere a siren wailed like the night itself was warning us to move.

Colt pulled back first, his lips damp from our kiss, his breathing heavier than the run had made it. He brushed his thumb over my cheekbone and then jerked his head toward the door.

"They'll sweep this block in five minutes. We're not waiting to get boxed in."

I nodded, trying to steady my legs as the heat from his touch clashed with the cold air.

We slipped out a side entrance and emerged into a narrow corridor of alleyways, the buildings leaning in like the city was holding its breath. Our footsteps splashed lightly in shallow puddles as Colt led the way, every muscle in his back tense beneath his soaked shirt.

A shadow moved.

He shoved me against the wall instinctively, his gun in his hand before I realized he'd drawn it.

"Scar's boys," he whispered.

Through the slant of rain, I saw three figures sweep the street with flashlights, guns hanging loose at their sides like casual threats. My pulse pounded in my ears.

Colt leaned in, so close I could feel his breath on my neck.

"When I move, follow. Don't stop. Don't even look back."

"I trust you," I whispered, and I meant it more than I wanted to admit.

The corner of his mouth twitched—just a flicker of something softer—before he slipped from the shadows, silent and deadly. He moved like a predator, cutting across the alley with calculated speed. I followed, lungs burning, heart slamming in my chest.

We darted into another side street, ducking behind a parked delivery van.

I crouched low, chest heaving, and Colt pressed a hand to my back, steady and grounding. But when his fingers lingered, stroking up along my spine, a different shiver ran through me.

"You keep running like that," he murmured, "and I'm gonna start thinking you like the chase."

I turned my head, meeting his gaze in the dim light. "Maybe I like what happens after."

His eyes darkened, and for a moment, danger was an aphrodisiac. His mouth found mine again, rougher this time, claiming. I opened to him, heat curling low in my stomach as his hand slid to my hip, thumb pressing just under the waistband of my shorts.

A shout cracked through the alley.

"Over there!"

We tore apart, sprinting before bullets could find us. The gunfire came anyway, echoing off the walls, each shot a spark in the night. We ducked behind the van, Colt firing back with calm precision.

The smell of gunpowder and rain filled my lungs, my body trembling with a cocktail of adrenaline and forbidden hunger. Even as fear spiked, the memory of his hands burned hotter than the chase itself.

He grabbed my wrist, and we bolted again, cutting through a fenced yard littered with rusted bikes and abandoned furniture. We didn't stop until we found another safe pocket of shadow, both of us panting, rainwater streaming down our faces.

Colt's hand was still gripping mine like he might never let go.

"You good?" he asked, scanning my face.

I nodded, though my pulse was still racing for more than one reason.

"Stay with me," he said, softer now, thumb brushing the back of my hand. "I'm not losing you tonight."

We crouched in the shadows of a half-collapsed shed, our breathing ragged. The city dripped and whispered around us, but the only sound I could really hear was Colt's heartbeat where our shoulders pressed together.

"They won't stop," I whispered.

"They never do," he said, scanning the alley with sharp eyes. "But neither do I."

He caught my chin and turned me toward him. Rain streaked his jaw, and the cut on his lip from earlier looked darker in the dim light. He leaned in, pressing a kiss to my mouth that tasted like danger and defiance. I melted into it, my hands clutching his soaked shirt, needing the heat he carried.

A metallic clang echoed somewhere nearby—Scar's crew overturning trash cans in their hunt.

Colt broke the kiss but stayed close, lips brushing mine as he whispered, "We move now, or we're done."

We slipped out the back of the shed and crept through the rain-glossed back streets. He led with sure steps, my hand tight in his, and I could feel the tremor in his grip—not fear, but restraint.

A chain-link fence blocked the next alley. Colt vaulted over like it was nothing, then reached down, gripping my waist to lift me. For one dizzy second, our bodies aligned, his hands firm on my hips, and I felt the electricity between us pulse stronger than the storm.

We landed in a narrow courtyard surrounded by abandoned buildings. A broken neon sign buzzed above, its pink light flickering across Colt's face.

"This'll do," he said, scanning the perimeter. "We can breathe for a second."

I pressed my back against the wall, heart still sprinting. "Are we safe?"

"Safe enough." He came to me, dripping wet, heat radiating off him despite the cold.

When he caged me against the wall with his arms, I didn't move away. My breath hitched as his hand traced the line of my jaw, sliding down to my throat, pausing there—not to control, but to feel the pulse racing beneath his touch.

"You're fire in a storm," he said, voice low and raw.

"And you're trouble I can't stay away from," I whispered.

The kiss that followed was molten, his mouth claiming mine with hunger and relief. I pulled him closer, feeling the tension in his body coil like a spring. His hands explored with reverent urgency, tracing wet curves and sliding beneath my shirt to warm my chilled skin.

A distant shout broke through the rain.

We froze.

"They're still sweeping," he murmured against my ear. "But we've got time for one secret."

His fingers tangled in my hair as his lips explored my throat, and I arched into him, biting back a gasp. The night pressed in on us, danger and desire braided tight. It was reckless, but it felt like surviving.

We finally pulled apart, breathless, the rain cooling our overheated skin. Colt rested his forehead against mine, his voice rough with both warning and promise.

"This city's a loaded clip," he said. "And you just pulled the trigger."

Chapter 3 Safehouse's and Silence–

The rain had stopped, leaving the streets slick and gleaming under the city's fractured neon glow. Colt's hand was still in mine, warm and strong, as if letting go might undo everything we'd survived in the last hour.

We moved cautiously through the alleyways, our soaked clothes clinging to our skin, the city's silence feeling heavier than the storm. Every sound— dripping gutters, a rattling trash lid—felt amplified.

"Scar's crew won't quit," Colt said, voice low but edged with steel. "They'll circle these blocks all night if they think I've got something worth bleeding for."

I squeezed his hand. "Do you?"

He glanced at me, a ghost of a smirk playing at his lips. "Maybe. Or maybe they're just too stupid to know I'm not the one you chase head-on."

We ducked into a derelict auto shop, the air thick with the smell of oil and rust. Moonlight spilled through a cracked skylight, painting Colt's face in pale silver. He leaned against the wall, finally exhaling like he'd been holding the city on his shoulders all night.

"You're shaking," he said, eyes flicking over me.

I hadn't even noticed until he said it—my hands were trembling, a mix of cold, adrenaline, and something hotter I didn't want to name.

"I'm fine," I said, hugging myself.

He stepped forward, brushing wet strands of hair from my face. His touch was grounding, and his voice softened.

"Don't lie to me, angel. I can read you better than the streets."

I wanted to argue, to throw up the walls I'd always lived behind, but his gaze pinned me in place. For a man who could kill without flinching, Colt's eyes held a kind of dangerous tenderness that unraveled me.

Then he kissed me.

Not the frantic, adrenaline-laced kiss from the alley. This one was slow, deep, and claiming—like he had all the time in the world even as danger pressed closer. His hands cupped my face, and I let myself melt into him, tasting rain and gunpowder on his lips.

My fingers tangled in his shirt, pulling him closer. When his palm slid along my hip, tracing the curve with deliberate slowness, a shiver shot up my spine. It was reckless, and yet I felt safer here in this ruined garage than I ever had in my own bed.

The creak of a floorboard snapped us apart.

Colt's gun was in his hand instantly, his body shifting to shield me as he scanned the shadows. I held my breath, the kiss still burning on my lips.

A stray cat darted across the floor, disappearing out the back door.

He exhaled, easing the tension just a fraction.

"This city doesn't sleep," he muttered. Then he glanced back at me, smirk tugging at his mouth. "Neither do we, apparently."

Colt didn't lower the gun right away. He prowled the edge of the shadows, every step silent, every movement calculated. The flicker of the broken neon from outside made his face look carved from steel—part protector, part predator.

I stayed near the wall, trying to slow my heartbeat. The kiss still tingled on my lips, and my body still hummed from his touch, but the memory of Scar's men hunting us outside kept my nerves sharp.

"Clear," Colt said finally, sliding the gun back into the holster at the small of his back. He turned to me, and just like that, the predator became something softer, something dangerously human.

"You're drenched." He tugged at the hem of my shirt, his knuckles brushing my stomach. "You'll catch a cold if we don't warm you up."

My laugh came out shaky. "That your excuse?"

He grinned—wolfish, unrepentant. "Do I need one?"

He shrugged off his jacket and draped it over my shoulders, the leather heavy and warm with his scent—gun oil, rain, and the faintest trace of smoke.

"You should take it," I murmured. "You're soaked too."

"I run hot." His gaze held mine like a challenge. "Besides, I like the way it looks on you."

When he stepped closer, I didn't back away. His thumb brushed along my lower lip, tracing where he'd kissed me before, and I felt the world narrow down to the space between us.

"Tell me to stop," he said, his voice rough with something rawer than desire.

I didn't.

His mouth claimed mine again, and the kiss deepened fast—urgent, hungry, like the storm outside had followed us in and wrapped us both in its electricity. My back hit the cool wall of the garage, and he pressed against me, heat radiating through soaked clothes.

His hands were skilled, reverent yet bold, sliding under the edge of the leather jacket to cup my waist, trace my spine. I gasped into his mouth as he found that spot just above my hip, and he swallowed the sound like a man starving.

I wasn't thinking about Scar or the streets or the danger waiting outside.

I was thinking about this man—this weapon—pressing every secret of his body into mine and making me feel like I'd stepped into the fire willingly.

When his lips trailed along my jaw to my neck, heat sparked low in my belly. He bit lightly, just enough to make me gasp again, and murmured against my skin,

"You taste like trouble, angel. Sweet trouble."

My fingers threaded through his damp hair as he lifted me slightly, my legs wrapping around him instinctively. He pressed me to the wall, the leather of his holster cool against my thigh, a stark reminder of the world we lived in.

Suddenly, the crash of glass shattered the moment.

Colt set me down instantly, gun drawn before the echo even died. My breath hitched as footsteps scuffed in the next room, heavier than a cat this time.

"They found us," he whispered, eyes locked on the shadows.

And just like that, the heat of the kiss turned to adrenaline again.

The crash echoed like a gunshot, and my pulse went wild. Colt signaled me to stay put with two fingers, his body low and lethal as he moved toward the shadows.

The wet streets outside had fallen silent—no engines, no voices—just the drip of rain from the broken gutter and the faint hum of neon through the window.

I forced myself to steady my breathing, even as the taste of him still lingered on my lips. Desire and fear were a dangerous cocktail, and in that moment, I was drunk on both.

A figure stepped into the moonlight of the garage—a man in a dark hoodie, pistol raised.

Colt didn't hesitate.

In one fluid motion, he grabbed the man's wrist, slammed it against the wall, and drove a fist into his ribs. The gun clattered to the floor. I bit back a scream as Colt twisted him around, pinning him.

"Where's Scar?" Colt's voice was ice.

The man groaned, gasping. "You think… I'd tell you?"

Colt pressed harder, and the man cried out.

"You've got three seconds before I find out the hard way," Colt said, his tone almost casual, which somehow made it scarier.

A second set of footsteps echoed from the stairwell.

I snatched the fallen pistol and leveled it with both hands like Colt had shown me before. My arms trembled, but I wasn't about to be the weak link.

A tall figure emerged—a woman this time, with a scar slicing across her cheek. Her smirk was pure malice.

"Well, well," she said. "Look at the lovebirds."

Colt didn't flinch. "Tell Scar he's losing his touch if he's sending rookies after me."

Her smirk faltered, replaced by a glint of irritation. "Rookie, huh?"

She raised her gun.

I didn't think. I fired.

The shot was deafening in the confined space. The woman staggered back, her gun clattering to the ground as she hit the wall. I didn't know if I'd hit her or just scared her, but adrenaline was burning through me like wildfire.

Colt kicked the first man away and grabbed my wrist. "Move!"

We bolted through the garage's back door, sprinting into the slick alley. The city smelled of wet asphalt and smoke, and somewhere in the distance, sirens began to wail.

We ran until the world was a blur of shadows and light, my hand locked in his like it was the only real thing left.

When we finally stopped, breathless, in the cover of another abandoned building, Colt spun me against the wall.

"You shot at her," he said, voice sharp with both awe and reprimand.

"She was going to shoot you," I fired back, adrenaline still shaking my hands.

He stared at me for a long moment, his chest heaving, water dripping from his hair. Then he kissed me hard, like he couldn't decide if he wanted to scold me or worship me.

"You're dangerous," he whispered against my mouth.

"Then we match," I said.

We stayed pressed against the crumbling brick wall for a long moment, catching our breath. The city hummed around us—sirens in the distance, rain whispering on metal rooftops—but here, in this narrow alley, it felt like the world had shrunk to just us.

Colt's hand cupped the back of my neck, warm and steady. "You all right?" he asked, voice low.

"I don't know," I admitted, my pulse still skittering. "I just... shot at someone."

"You saved me," he said simply. "That's all I see when I look at you."

His words hit me harder than the danger had. Nobody had ever said something like that to me—so raw, so certain.

He led me into the shelter of an abandoned row house, where a broken window let in streaks of moonlight. It smelled like dust and old rain, but it was dry, and for now, it was ours.

Colt shrugged off his wet shirt, the muscles in his shoulders rippling as he wrung it out. My eyes betrayed me, tracing the scars that mapped his chest, each one a secret story he hadn't told yet.

He caught me staring. "See something you like?"

I should have been embarrassed, but instead I stepped closer, fingertips hovering over a jagged line along his ribs. "These are all real?"

He nodded. "Every one of them a lesson." His voice dropped, rough and intimate. "Some lessons I don't want you to ever have to learn."

I touched his skin finally, warm under my fingertips, and he closed his eyes for a beat like he could feel me beneath the surface.

"I'm not afraid," I whispered.

He opened his eyes, and the look there stole my breath. Not just desire—something deeper, something like a storm he'd been holding back for years.

When he kissed me this time, it wasn't frantic like before. It was slow, deliberate, a claiming and a promise all in one. His hands mapped my body with reverence, like he needed to memorize me before the world stole the moment away.

Clothes became an afterthought. The wet jacket slid from my shoulders, and he laid me gently on the old wooden floor, cushioning me with his shirt. Moonlight painted his face as he hovered above me, and for a second, the danger outside felt like a different universe.

Every touch was deliberate—his lips tracing my collarbone, his fingers curling against my hip, the warmth of his body grounding me in a reality that felt like fire and gravity colliding. He whispered things against my skin—dark, tender promises I wasn't sure I should believe, but wanted to.

When he finally moved inside me, it wasn't just heat—it was connection, raw and consuming, a quiet storm that built slow until it had to break.

Afterward, we lay tangled on the floor, the sound of our breathing mingling with the rain outside. My cheek rested against his chest, and I could feel his heartbeat—steady, protective, alive.

"You're in this now," he said softly, tracing circles along my spine. "There's no turning back."

"I don't want to," I murmured.

His hand stilled for a moment, and I felt the weight of his unspoken thoughts. For now, he let them drift into the quiet, and we stayed that way—warmth and vulnerability wrapped up in the heart of a city that wanted us dead.

Chapter 4 –One Bullet Left

Morning came softly, like the city had forgotten who we were for a few stolen hours. The first light slid through the broken window, painting Colt's skin in gold, highlighting every line of muscle and the shadows of his scars.

I woke to the sound of his heartbeat beneath my cheek. Warmth cocooned me for a moment, the scent of rain-damp wood and his cologne grounding me in a place that felt safe, though I knew better.

"You watchin' me sleep?" His voice was rough, teasing, low enough that it vibrated against my ear.

"Maybe," I whispered, letting my fingers trace the line of his jaw. "It's the only time you look… peaceful."

His eyes opened, dark and sharp even in the soft light. "Peaceful ain't a word people use for me." He rolled onto his side, his hand sliding up my thigh, his touch slow and deliberate. "But I'll take it from you."

I leaned into him, lips brushing his collarbone, tasting salt and the ghost of last night. His fingers tangled in my hair, a shiver running through me as he deepened the kiss, taking his time like the world outside didn't exist.

For a fleeting moment, it was just us—breath and skin and the dangerous kind of comfort that made me want to believe in forever.

Then, a sharp metallic clatter broke the spell. Both of us froze.

Colt's expression shifted instantly, the predator awake in his eyes. He sat up in one fluid motion, pulling me with him. "Get dressed. Now."

I grabbed my jeans and shirt, hands shaking as I slipped them on. He moved with silent efficiency, tucking a pistol into the back of his waistband and sliding a knife into his boot.

The sound came again, this time closer—a scrape along the hallway floor, like someone dragging metal.

Colt pressed a finger to his lips and pointed to the dark corner by the window. I crouched there, heart pounding against my ribs, trying to make myself small.

The door creaked open.

A shadow spilled across the floor, tall and heavy.

"Check in there," a man's voice said, deep and rough.

A second figure stepped into the room, and in that instant, Colt struck.

The room erupted in violence—fast, silent, lethal. Colt caught the man's arm, yanked him off balance, and drove him into the wall with a bone-crunching thud. The second man lunged, but Colt spun him into a chokehold, his movements fluid and precise, like a dance of survival.

I couldn't move, couldn't breathe. This wasn't the Colt I touched in the moonlight last night—this was the man who lived in the shadows, a weapon in human form.

The first man groaned on the floor, and Colt's voice dropped to a growl.

"Who sent you?"

"Scar… wants her…" The man's eyes darted toward me.

The words hit me like a slap of ice.

Colt didn't hesitate—he knocked him unconscious with a swift blow, then turned to me, jaw tight.

"They're done playing."

Colt's eyes flicked toward the window, then the doorway. He was calculating. Always calculating.

"They know where we are," he said, his voice calm in a way that made my skin prickle. "We can't stay."

Another noise came from downstairs—a door slamming open, footsteps pounding against warped wood.

"Backup," I whispered.

"Yeah." Colt's jaw flexed. "Scar sent more than two."

He reached for my hand, pulling me to my feet, and his touch was steady, commanding. My legs shook, but when he squeezed my fingers, I felt some of that steadiness transfer into me.

"We move fast, stay low, and if I tell you to run—you run. Don't look back."

"I'm not leaving you," I said, breathless but firm.

He looked at me then, really looked, like he was weighing the truth in my words against the danger closing in. Something in his expression softened for a fraction of a second.

"Then stay on me."

We slipped into the hallway. The house creaked under our weight, the old floorboards betraying us with every cautious step. Down below, men's voices echoed—rough, sharp, and too close.

"...check the back rooms!"

"...Scar said don't let her get away!"

Every word was a nail driven into my spine.

Colt led us toward the back stairwell, moving with the predatory silence of someone who had lived too long in danger's shadow. I tried to mimic his steps, but my heart was a drum in my chest, loud enough I was sure they could hear it.

He paused at the landing and pulled me flush against the wall, his lips brushing my ear.

"Three of them. Armed. Wait for my signal."

His whisper burned like fire, and in the middle of fear, heat coiled in my stomach. The intimacy of survival was a different kind of closeness—a heartbeat away from life or death.

A shadow crossed the lower stair.

Colt moved first, his body a blur of precision. He grabbed the first man by the collar, yanked him upward, and slammed the butt of his gun into the side of his skull. The man crumpled before he could even cry out.

The second one turned, raising his weapon—

I reacted without thinking. My hand closed around the old metal pipe leaning in the corner, and I swung hard. The crack echoed like a gunshot, and the man dropped his gun as he stumbled back.

Colt finished him with a clean, brutal strike that left him sprawled across the stairs.

But the third man was ready.

He fired, and the bullet ripped through the wall inches from my face.

"Move!" Colt barked, pulling me toward the back door.

We crashed through it into the alley, the morning air cold and sharp against my skin. Rainwater splashed under my shoes, and the city came alive in all the worst ways—sirens, echoing shouts, the growl of a black SUV turning the corner.

"They're still coming," I said, breath ragged.

"Good." Colt's lips twisted into a dangerous half-smile. "Let 'em."

He grabbed my hand again, and we ran into the maze of backstreets, the city swallowing us in its wet, glittering teeth.

The alley twisted into another, narrower one, the wet pavement shining under a weak morning sun. My lungs burned, and every shadow felt alive.

Colt slowed only when we ducked behind a dumpster, pressed into the cold brick wall. He held me close, his palm over my mouth, our bodies flush, as an SUV rumbled past the mouth of the alley.

I could feel his heart pounding against my chest—fast, wild, alive.

When the engine noise faded, he released my mouth but not my waist.

"You okay?" His voice was low, rough, still laced with the edge of violence.

I nodded, but my breath trembled. "I… I think so."

He tilted his head, studying me. Rain dripped from his hair onto my face, mingling with the heat between us. "You didn't freeze. You fought."

"You would've died if I hadn't." My voice was sharper than I intended, but it was the truth.

His eyes softened with something raw and unspoken. "You keep surprising me."

We stayed pressed together in the shadows, bodies still humming with adrenaline. I realized, in that stillness, how close we were. How close we *always* seemed to end up.

His thumb brushed my lower lip—slow, deliberate—and I felt my whole body react, heat spiraling low in my stomach.

"You scared?" he asked.

"Yes," I whispered.

"Good. Fear keeps you sharp." He leaned closer, his breath warm against my ear. "But right now… I can't stop thinking about last night."

His hand slid down my back, over the curve of my hip, and for a heartbeat, the danger faded under the gravity between us. My lips found his without hesitation, and the kiss was desperate, messy, alive.

It tasted like rain, like fear and desire tangled together.

A shout shattered the moment.

"Down there!"

We broke apart as footsteps splashed through the street behind us. Colt's grip tightened on my hand.

"Rooftops. Only chance now."

He boosted me up onto a rusted fire escape ladder, his palms firm and sure on my thighs, sending a thrill through me even as panic pulsed in my veins. I scrambled up, Colt following in a fluid motion.

By the time the men reached the alley, we were already halfway up the fire escape, pressed against the metal in silence.

"They went this way!" one of them yelled.

Colt's eyes met mine, and for a second, even with danger below, I felt… invincible with him.

We climbed higher, into the city's jagged skyline, chasing survival and something far more dangerous than bullets.

The city stretched out in every direction, a wet, glimmering labyrinth under the weak morning sun. Steam curled from vents, and puddles on the rooftop reflected the jagged skyline like shards of broken glass.

We crouched behind an old ventilation unit, listening to the footsteps and shouts below echo off the alley walls. My breath caught on every sound.

Colt crouched next to me, his pistol resting against his thigh. Calm, always calm, like chaos only sharpened him.

"They'll sweep the rooftops next," he said, voice low. "We need to move when they fan out. Until then, we wait."

I hugged my knees to my chest, the cold metal under me biting through my jeans. "What if they… catch us?"

41

His gaze cut to me, dark and unreadable. "Then I put them in the ground before they put us there."

The casual weight of his words sent a shiver through me. Not just fear—something hotter, heavier. The same thing that always pulled me to him, no matter how many times I swore I'd keep my distance.

We sat in silence for a moment, the air between us thick with danger and something else— something intimate.

Colt shifted closer, his shoulder brushing mine. The contact was slight, but it was enough to make my pulse race.

"You okay?" he asked, softer this time.

"I don't know." My voice shook, betraying the cocktail of adrenaline and desire threading through me. "I... I've never been this close to—"

"Death?" He gave a half-smile, dark and knowing. "It makes everything sharper. Every sound, every touch... every kiss."

He leaned in, and I let him. Our lips met with a slow, burning intensity that felt different from last night's desperation. This was deeper, heavier—like the city could collapse beneath us and we'd still be tangled up in each other, claiming life in the face of death.

His hand slid to my jaw, tilting my face to his. My heart pounded so hard I thought it would echo across the rooftops. I melted into the kiss, the taste of rain and danger on his lips, and for a moment, the world narrowed to just this: us, alive, wanting, invincible.

A metallic clang snapped us back.

Voices. Closer.

"They're up here!"

Colt broke the kiss, eyes flashing with steel. "Time to move."

He grabbed my hand, and we darted across the rooftop, the city wind whipping around us. A ladder led to the next building, and he helped me down first, his hand lingering on my waist even in the rush.

By the time we hit the lower roof, gunfire cracked behind us, bullets sparking against the rusted metal where we'd just been.

We ran. Together. Hearts pounding in sync, tethered by fear and something far more dangerous than the men chasing us.

And in that moment, I realized the truth that terrified me almost as much as Scar's men did:

I would follow Colt anywhere.

Even if it killed me.

Chapter 5 No Exit Wounds

We stumbled into the safehouse just as the sky cracked open with rain. The old warehouse smelled of rust and oil, and water dripped from the ceiling in a slow, steady rhythm. Colt bolted the steel door behind us, and for the first time since dawn, I let out a shaky breath.

"You're safe," he said, though his eyes never stopped scanning the dark corners of the room. "For now."

I leaned against the wall, soaked to the bone, my pulse still racing from the rooftop chase. "Safe," I echoed, though it didn't feel true. My body hummed with leftover adrenaline and the ghost of his kiss.

He crossed the room and crouched in front of a crate, pulling out a clean towel and a first-aid kit. "Sit."

I hesitated, then perched on the edge of a workbench. He knelt between my knees, the heat of him cutting through the damp chill, and gently wiped blood from a scrape on my shin. His touch was careful, deliberate, almost tender—so different from the man who'd shot two men in cold blood hours ago.

"You're bleeding," he said.

"Just a scratch."

"You're shaking."

"Not from fear."

His dark eyes flicked up to mine, and the air shifted again—charged, dangerous. His hand brushed higher on my thigh, and a tremor of want rolled through me, hot and electric.

The door creaked.

Colt froze. His hand went to his gun.

Then the shadows moved, and someone stepped out from behind the stacked pallets.

I recognized the face instantly—Tino. Colt's so-called ally. He'd driven us once, kept watch another night, even handed me a mug of coffee with a smirk that felt almost brotherly.

"Relax," Tino said, raising his hands. Rain dripped from his jacket. "I tracked you here to make sure you were good."

Colt didn't lower his weapon. "How the hell did you find this place?"

"Man, you think I don't know all your hideouts? I've been covering you for years." He stepped closer, slow and easy. "Figured you'd need backup."

I wanted to believe him. I *almost* did—until Colt's body went rigid next to me. His gun didn't waver, but his voice dropped to something lethal.

"Backup doesn't come with a tail," he said.

Tino hesitated. Blinked.

Then smiled.

It wasn't the smile I knew. It was sharp, cold, and cruel.

"You were never supposed to make it off that roof, Colt," he said. "Scar's done playing nice."

The air snapped tight.

My stomach dropped, a cold rush of betrayal washing over me as the reality set in—this wasn't a rescue.

This was an execution.

The room went dead quiet except for the drip-drip-drip of water hitting the concrete floor.

Colt didn't blink, didn't breathe, gun trained squarely on Tino.

"You picked the wrong side," Colt said, voice like gravel.

Tino tilted his head, grin widening. "No, Colt. *You* did. Scar's got the streets sewn up, and you're still running solo like it's ten years ago. Times change. Money talks."

"And you sold me out for pocket change?"

"Not just you." His eyes slid toward me, and the smile turned into something uglier. "Scar wanted the girl. Said she's the key to keeping you in line."

My chest tightened. "What?"

Colt moved, quick as a strike. He shoved me behind him, his body a wall of heat and danger. "Over my dead body."

Tino chuckled. "Yeah. That's the plan."

The gunshot was almost too fast to register.

Colt had fired first.

Tino dove behind a stack of pallets, and the bullet splintered wood where his head had been. The warehouse erupted into chaos—gunfire cracking, echoing off the walls, the metallic scent of gunpowder filling the air.

"Stay down!" Colt barked.

I dropped behind the workbench, heart hammering. My ears rang as Tino's shots ripped through the shadows, one grazing the metal inches from my head.

Colt moved like a predator—fluid, precise—using every piece of cover as he closed the distance.

But Tino was fast, darting in and out, his laughter bouncing off the walls.

"You're slipping, Colt!" Tino taunted. "Scar was right—your heart's a liability!"

Then I saw it.

A flicker of movement above—Tino climbing a side ladder to the mezzanine. He had the high ground now, his gun aimed directly at Colt's back.

"Colt!" I screamed.

He spun just as the shot rang out.

It missed—barely—but the ricochet sent sparks across the concrete. Colt dove behind an overturned table, cursing under his breath.

"Think fast, lover boy!" Tino shouted, voice dripping with mockery. "You've got one shot at walking out alive—leave the girl, and maybe I let you crawl away."

Colt's answer was another bullet, this one so close Tino yelped and ducked behind the railing.

The tension snapped like a live wire. I could *feel* Colt's rage vibrating off him, as if this betrayal had cut deeper than any bullet ever could.

He motioned for me to stay down, then began stalking the shadows with murder in his eyes.

This was no longer a fight.

It was a hunt.

The warehouse had gone dark except for the flickering overhead light swaying like a dying heartbeat. Smoke drifted through the beams, curling in the air like ghosts of the lives this building used to house. Colt moved with surgical precision, but Tino

47

was no rookie—he was bred in the same war-torn streets, taught by the same wolves.

I watched from behind the metal tool rack, heart racing, barely daring to breathe. Colt had disappeared into the far shadows, using silence as a weapon. The only thing louder than the creaking metal was the thud of my pulse.

A crash sounded above. Colt fired once—twice—but the bullets punched holes in the platform. Tino ducked and returned fire, the shots wild, one zipping past my cheek close enough to burn.

Colt moved again, fast, cornering him like a predator.

But Tino was already slipping through a busted window at the top level, feet scraping against the rusted ledge.

"No!" Colt shouted, sprinting up the side steps, but it was too late.

Tino hurled himself out the window.

Colt reached the edge seconds later, gun drawn. "I got a clean shot," he muttered. "I got it."

He didn't fire.

Below, Tino limped through the alley, disappearing into the city fog. He was bleeding, but he was grinning.

"He's gonna run straight to Scar," I said, stepping beside him.

Colt didn't look at me. His jaw was clenched so tight I could see the muscle twitch.

"I should've killed him," he said, low and bitter. "But he was my brother once."

Downstairs, silence stretched like a loaded weapon between us. Colt descended the stairs slowly, every step heavier than the last.

"We're not safe now," I said, needing to break the quiet. "They'll know where we are."

"I know." He knelt beside the gear bag, tossing a pistol onto the table. "We move tonight."

My voice cracked. "Where?"

"Doesn't matter." He paused, then looked at me. "So long as it's together."

We stood in the wreckage of the only place that had felt like shelter in days, the walls now echoing with betrayal. The storm outside pounded harder, the city roaring louder. But inside, for a breath, it was just the two of us—our trust cracked, but not broken.

I reached for him.

He didn't flinch.

Location: The Oracle Room, Second Floor of Black Crescent Casino

The room was dim, scented with cigar smoke and expensive betrayal.

Scar stood with his back to the curved glass, overlooking the casino floor below. Neon lights flashed against his dark tailored suit, reflecting like warning sirens across his gold watch and the blade of the small knife he cleaned with meticulous care.

Tino sat across from him, shoulder bandaged, lip split, one eye already purpling. A whiskey glass trembled in his bloodied hands.

"You lost them," Scar said flatly, still not turning to face him.

49

"I—I had them, boss. I had Colt in the sightline. I swear. But he's like a ghost. Slippery as ever."

"Ghosts don't bleed, Tino. You do."

Scar finally turned, slow and deliberate. His eyes were ice—dead and precise. He set the knife down with a soft *click*.

"He hesitated," Tino added quickly, a desperate edge in his voice. "He didn't kill me. That means something. He's slipping. Getting soft for the girl."

Scar raised an eyebrow. "The girl…"

"Yeah. She's the reason he's off-balance. I saw it. She screams, he flinches. He's never flinched for *anyone*, boss."

Scar reached for the deck of cards resting on the table. With the ease of a magician, he spread them out, fanned them, selected one, and flipped it over.

The Queen of Spades.

He stared at it for a long time.

"So, the girl's the weakness," he murmured. "Noted."

He lit a cigar, exhaled smoke like a prophet. "What did I tell you when I brought you in from the cold, Tino?"

Tino's throat worked. "You said blood makes us family, but loyalty makes us live."

"And yet, here you are—dragging failure into my room, hoping blood will be enough." Scar gestured toward the Queen card. "You let that woman become a problem. That's on you."

Tino stood, maybe to defend himself, maybe to run.

Scar nodded once.

From the shadows, a man in all black emerged, silent as a reaper.

There was no time to scream.

One gunshot.

Tino dropped to the floor.

Scar didn't flinch.

He turned to the man in black.

"Find the girl. Strip her from Colt like flesh from bone. And when he comes to collect her…"

He smiled now, slow and cruel.

"…break him."

Chapter 6 Unloaded Lies

The cab reeked of cheap incense and regret. Colt had slipped the driver a thick wad of bills and a made-up name, and neither of us had spoken since.

Outside the cracked window, the city blurred—neon signs bleeding into puddles, headlights slicing through mist like blades. Every corner we passed felt like it could be the last. The silence between us wasn't cold. It was coiled. Loaded.

Colt's thigh pressed against mine in the backseat, steady, warm, but his jaw was tight, teeth grinding. I could feel the weight in him—the storm behind his eyes, the guilt he hadn't said aloud.

"You should've let me go," I whispered, breaking the silence.

His head turned slowly toward me. "That's not who I am."

"But I'm why they're hunting you now."

"You're wrong," he said, voice gravel. "They were always hunting me. You're just the part I'll kill to protect."

I swallowed hard. My fingers itched to reach for him, to pull him closer and say something soft to counter the sharp world closing in around us. But I didn't. Because softness, right now, might shatter us both.

The cab slowed in front of a run-down motel tucked behind a liquor store and a shuttered pawn shop. It looked forgotten. Safe, in the way that only places no one wants to remember could be.

Colt paid in cash. No names. No paper trail.

Love is a Loaded Clip

The moment we stepped into the room, the air shifted. Peeling wallpaper, a stained mattress, one buzzing lamp. Still, the door locked. The curtains closed. The world went silent again.

Colt sat on the edge of the bed, running a hand through his damp hair. I dropped my jacket, every muscle screaming, and stood there watching him—watching the way his shoulders carried weight like they'd forgotten anything else.

"Why didn't you kill him?" I asked.

His eyes flicked up to mine. "Because once... I thought Tino was family."

I crossed the room slowly, the floor creaking under my bare feet. "And now?"

"Now he's Scar's dog. And I'll put him down."

He looked up at me then, and something broke open behind his gaze—exhaustion, pain... need.

"I can't lose you," he said.

"You haven't."

He reached for me.

And I didn't hesitate.

The silence wrapped around us like a second skin, thick with what hadn't been said. My fingers grazed Colt's knuckles—just a brush—and even that sent heat rippling beneath my skin.

He looked at me like I was the only light left in his war-torn world.

His hand rose to my waist, calloused fingers sliding beneath my shirt, tentative at first. But I didn't stop him. I leaned in, pressing my forehead to his.

"Tell me this is real," I whispered.

53

"It's the only thing that is," he breathed, lips brushing mine.

When he kissed me, it was slow—like he didn't know if we had minutes or seconds left. His mouth was warm, reverent, but still hungry, like he needed to memorize every inch of me with taste alone.

My fingers tangled in his shirt, yanking it upward. I wanted him closer. Wanted skin against skin, no past between us—no blood, no betrayals. Just now.

He pulled the shirt over his head, eyes never leaving mine. There were old scars across his ribs, each one a secret he hadn't shared. I traced them with my fingertips, and he shivered.

"You're shaking," I murmured.

"Not from fear," he echoed, voice rough.

I climbed into his lap, legs straddling him, and kissed him again—deeper this time, desperate. His hands roamed my body, slow but certain, as if every curve had already lived in his memory.

There was no rush. No performance. Just us.

The way his thumb skimmed my jaw before trailing down my throat… the way he undressed me with care, pausing to kiss each inch of exposed skin… the way I whispered his name like it was a vow.

He laid me back on the creaky bed, covering my body with his, and the world outside ceased to exist. No Scar. No Tino. No threats.

Only heat and breath and aching relief.

When he entered me, it wasn't a conquest. It was surrender—mine and his. A silent agreement to live in this moment, even if the next one tried to destroy us.

We moved together, lips brushing, hands clinging, breath catching. And when I came undone beneath him, he whispered my name like a promise he would never break.

Later, I lay curled against his chest, his heartbeat steady beneath my cheek.

"You're not just something I'm trying to protect," he said into my hair. "You're the reason I want out."

My eyes stung, but I didn't cry.

Not yet.

Because in this room, with him wrapped around me, I still had hope.

Colt had just started to drift off, arms still folded protectively around me, when the soft *buzz* of his burner phone broke the quiet.

He stiffened. Reached for it.

Blocked number.

One message.

"Nice room. Shame it's not fireproof."

He barely had time to curse before the window shattered.

A brick flew through it, crashing into the wall, shards of glass flying like razors. Smoke immediately followed—thick, black, chemical.

Colt sprang into motion, grabbing the gun from the nightstand, pulling me from the bed in one swift move. I coughed, eyes burning, vision blurring from the sudden gas flooding the room.

"Bathroom—go!" he barked.

We stumbled in, slamming the door just as flames licked across the carpet outside. The motel wasn't just being watched—it was being torched.

Colt ripped the shower curtain down, wrapped it around me. "Stay low, stay breathing."

I wanted to scream, but my training—my instinct—kicked in. Panic later. Survive now.

He slammed the butt of the gun against the tiny window above the tub until it cracked. Once. Twice. On the third hit, it shattered.

Smoke was rolling in faster now, turning everything orange-red and blinding.

Colt boosted me up. "Go!"

"But—"

"Now, Nay!"

I climbed through the broken frame, knees scraping the edges. The cold night air slapped me in the face like a wake-up call. I dropped down into an alley full of shadows and rot.

Seconds later, Colt followed—half-dressed, bleeding from the forearm, teeth clenched.

The fire roared behind us, devouring everything.

"They were watching," I gasped. "This whole time—"

"They never lost us," he said, voice hollow. "We didn't run fast enough."

He grabbed my hand and pulled me deeper into the alley, disappearing into the shadows before the first sirens pierced the night.

We didn't stop running until our legs gave out. Didn't speak until we reached a rooftop two blocks away, breathing hard, sweat mixing with smoke.

Colt scanned the horizon. "Scar's not playing anymore."

"What now?" I asked.

He looked at me, chest still heaving. "Now? We stop hiding."

The rooftop was cracked tar and forgotten pigeon feathers, barely wide enough for both of us to sit. Wind whipped around us, still thick with smoke from the burning motel.

Colt stared out over the city like it owed him something. Maybe it did.

I pulled the stolen hoodie tighter around me, still tasting ash. "You gonna keep running me through hell blind, or you finally gonna tell me who the hell Scar is to you?"

He flinched—not visibly, but I saw it in his hands, the way they clenched and relaxed.

"You already know the basics," he muttered. "He runs half the East Side. Launders through the Crescent. Makes ghosts of people who ask too many questions."

I shifted closer, tone sharper. "That's not what I asked."

He finally looked at me. "He's the reason I left the life."

"And now?"

"Now he's the reason I'm back in it."

I stood. "I can't keep getting dragged through this if I don't know what it is. You act like you're saving me—but you're the one with the kill order on your back. Who *was* Scar to you, Colt?"

Silence.

He exhaled like the truth was poison.

"He raised me."

I blinked. "What?"

Colt stood now too, shadows cutting across his jaw. "I was fifteen. Fresh outta lockup, nowhere to go. He found me. Gave me a gun, a job, a crew. Tino was like a brother. We ran numbers, moved product, cleaned messes."

"And then?"

"I killed the wrong man for the right reason," he said, voice low. "Scar said I went off-script. Told me loyalty didn't mean questioning the playbook."

"So you dipped."

"I ran. Took intel with me. Set fire to one of his stash houses. He made me a target that day."

My arms crossed. "So I'm what—collateral in a vendetta?"

"You're the only thing that ain't a weapon in this mess," he said, stepping closer. "But I'm starting to think maybe you're the only thing keeping me from turning into what he raised me to be."

My throat tightened. "You think that's romantic?"

"No," he said simply. "I think it's survival."

I stared at him, heat building behind my eyes. "Don't lie to me again, Colt. Don't think protecting me means hiding from me."

He nodded once. "I won't."

I stepped into him, pressing my forehead to his. His hand slid to the back of my neck. The city roared below, but here... it was just us.

No lies. No shields.

Just breath and fire and something real enough to burn for.

Chapter 7 –Trigger Discipline

The city never really slept. It just crouched low, breathing in shadows, waiting for the next scream or siren to wake it again. From the rooftop, I could feel the heartbeat of it—raw and restless, pulsing through the metal vents and cracked tar beneath my sneakers.

Colt had finally dozed, his back against the concrete ledge, a gun balanced across his thigh like an extension of his body. Even asleep, he radiated tension. I knew the second I moved too far, his eyes would snap open and his body would coil to strike.

But tonight, I didn't need saving. I needed control.

I crept across the roof toward the emergency ladder, my hoodie pulled tight against the night wind. The motel fire still painted the sky in an ugly orange smear in the distance, reminding me how close we'd come to becoming ghosts in Scar's story. I wasn't going to wait for Colt to decide our next move.

My life before him hadn't been innocent. I'd grown up watching my mom barter rent with favors and watching men crawl out of our apartment like secrets no one wanted. I'd learned early that survival was an art, and people underestimated girls who knew how to make themselves small until they needed to be dangerous.

The ladder screeched under my weight, and I cringed at the sound. A few blocks over, a bodega kept its neon "OPEN" sign glowing like a beacon.

That was where I'd start. Not for snacks—though my stomach gnawed at itself—but for information. I had someone I could call. Someone Colt didn't know about.

The streets were wet, slick with yesterday's rain and tonight's blood. Streetlights caught the puddles and threw their reflections back in gold streaks. I moved fast but casual, the way city girls do when they want to look invisible.

A homeless man muttered something about ghosts as I passed, and I didn't know if he meant me or the world chasing me.

Inside the bodega, the hum of the fridge and the faint smell of frying oil were weirdly comforting. The owner—a stocky Dominican man with a scar over his eyebrow—nodded at me.

"You look like trouble," he said in Spanish.

"Only the kind that pays," I replied, slipping him a folded twenty.

He smirked and slid his burner phone across the counter.

I dialed a number I hadn't touched in months.

"Who the hell—" The voice on the other end paused, then softened. "Nay?"

"Yeah, Rico. It's me."

"Girl, last I heard, you were running clean. You calling me means you ain't anymore."

I glanced out the window, making sure no shadows moved in the alley. "I need two things. A car no one's looking for and something... heavy. Preferably something that roars if anyone gets cute."

He whistled low. "That bad?"

"Worse."

A pause. I could hear the sound of a lighter flicking, smoke being exhaled. "You working with him again? The ghost with the gun?"

I hesitated. "I'm not working for him. I'm… with him."

He laughed once, dark and knowing. "Girl, you just marked yourself. Alright, I'll send a location. Two blocks east, old garage by the tracks. You got twenty minutes before I ghost."

"Gracias, Rico."

I hung up, slid the phone back, and left the bodega, moving quick. My pulse was hammering, not from fear but from something sharper—control. For once, I wasn't just the girl Colt saved. I was the one making moves that would keep us breathing.

I was halfway back to the rooftop when Colt appeared from the shadows. He didn't shout. He didn't curse. He just fell into step beside me like a storm cloud.

"You're lucky I didn't put a bullet in you," he said flatly.

"You were sleeping. I handled it."

His jaw tightened. "Handled what?"

"I got us a car. And guns. And maybe a little respect back."

He stopped walking, forcing me to turn and face him. His eyes were dark, unreadable. "You think this is a game, Nay? You disappear on me, you make yourself bait. Scar would've gutted you and left me the note."

I didn't back down. "Then maybe I'm done being the scared girl hiding behind your gun. You're not the only one who knows how to survive."

The silence between us crackled, hot and dangerous. Then, to my surprise, the corner of his mouth twitched. Not a smile, exactly, but maybe the ghost of one.

"Alright," he said. "Show me where we're going."

By the time we reached the garage, the streets felt quieter, like the city was holding its breath. A single bulb lit the space inside, casting long shadows over rusted cars and oil-stained concrete. Rico stood by a black Impala that purred like a secret. Beside it, a duffel bag sat on the hood.

"You got five minutes," he said. "And if anyone asks, I never saw you."

Colt unzipped the bag. Inside were two handguns, a sawed-off shotgun, extra clips, and a few burner phones.

"This will do," Colt said, inspecting the gear.

Rico's gaze shifted to me. "I hope you know what you're doing, chica. Men like him... they break everything they touch."

I glanced at Colt, then back at Rico. "Maybe he finally touched something that breaks back."

Colt's eyes lingered on me in a way that was equal parts warning and worship.

We left with the Impala, the duffel, and a whole new weight between us. I was done being just the girl in his story. This time, I was writing my own line in blood and smoke.

The Impala's engine growled like a caged animal as Colt guided it through the city's veins. Rain had returned in a soft drizzle, painting the streets in liquid mirrors, turning every passing light into a streak of gold or neon blood. I sat in the passenger seat, barefoot, my knees pulled close, still wrapped in the hoodie that smelled faintly of smoke and him.

We didn't talk for the first few blocks.

The weight of everything unsaid was heavier than the shotgun resting across Colt's lap.

The city opened like a secret map as we moved deeper, past shuttered bodegas, corner churches, and the old factories that sat hollow and hungry. This was the underbelly—the part of the city no tourist saw, no cop patrolled without backup, and no one survived without knowing who owned which block.

I broke the silence first, my voice quiet but sharp. "Where are we going?"

"Somewhere Scar won't look first," Colt said. "And somewhere I can get eyes on him before he sees me coming."

"You're planning a counterattack?"

He glanced at me, rainwater catching in the cut of his jaw. "You make it sound like a war."

"Isn't it?"

He didn't answer, but the way his fingers drummed against the steering wheel said enough.

The Impala turned down a narrower street, lined with chain-link fences and graffiti-stained brick. A mural of a girl with angel wings, half-faded, watched us pass. Her eyes felt like they were judging me, whispering, *You knew what he was, and you came anyway.*

I tried to push the thought down, but the silence made it grow.

"You don't trust me," I said finally.

Colt's jaw flexed. "I trust you to survive. That's different."

"Then start trusting me to fight."

He shot me a look, the kind that could cut a person in half if they weren't ready for it. "You already put yourself on the line tonight. One wrong alley and you're gone, Nay. Scar doesn't forgive mistakes. He buries them."

"I'm not afraid of him."

"You should be."

His voice was low, dangerous, and honest in a way that made my skin prickle. It wasn't condescension—it was fear disguised as command. But I was past being handled.

We slid into the parking lot of a building that looked abandoned, three stories of brick with boarded-up windows and a rusted metal door. Colt killed the lights and scanned the perimeter before cutting the engine.

"This where we die?" I asked, trying to keep my voice light.

He smirked, faint but real. "Nah. This is where we make sure he does."

He got out first, gun drawn, and motioned for me to follow. Inside, the air smelled like damp wood and old machinery. Shafts of moonlight cut through the broken roof panels, catching dust and dripping water.

"This used to be one of Scar's old drop sites," Colt said, checking corners. "He abandoned it a couple years back when the city started redeveloping the east docks."

"So why are we here?"

"Because he'll assume I'm too smart to come back." His smirk turned grim. "Sometimes being stupid on purpose is the smartest move."

We set up camp on the second floor, overlooking the street through a gap in the boarded windows. Colt laid out the weapons from Rico's duffel: the two pistols, the shotgun, extra clips, a knife that gleamed like it had a memory of blood.

He handled each piece with reverence. I watched his hands, steady even after fire, betrayal, and near death.

"You've done this before," I said.

He met my eyes. "More times than I should've survived."

There was no pride in his voice. Just a bone-deep exhaustion, the kind you carried in your soul.

I moved closer, close enough to touch him. "Then let me in. Stop locking me out of your head."

He hesitated, then finally said, "I don't wanna see you become me."

"You won't," I whispered. "But I also won't survive this if you keep treating me like I'm breakable."

For a moment, neither of us moved. Rain ticked against the broken glass. Somewhere far off, a siren wailed. Then he reached out, slid a pistol across the floor toward me.

"If you're in, you're in. No halfway."

I picked it up. It was heavy, cold, and alive in my hands. "I'm in."

The intimacy of that moment wasn't in the kiss we didn't share or the words we didn't say. It was in the way he finally trusted me with his life—truly, not just in the shadows of a motel room.

We spent the next hour in quiet preparation. I walked the perimeter with him, memorizing exits and blind spots. We rigged a couple of empty glass bottles on the stairwell as makeshift alarms, and Colt showed me how to load the shotgun without fumbling. His hands brushed mine more than once, heat sparking in the cold space.

By the time we settled back against the wall to watch the street, the city had gone quieter. Predatory quiet.

"This is the part I hate most," he said, voice a low rumble. "The waiting."

I rested my head against his shoulder. "Then let's make it worth it."

Somewhere below, a car door slammed.

Colt's eyes snapped open from their half-lidded rest. His hand tightened on the shotgun.

"Showtime," he whispered.

And just like that, the world tilted back into danger.

The first hint of trouble wasn't the car door— it was the silence after.

The kind of silence that pressed against your chest, making the air feel heavier, like the city itself was holding its breath.

Colt crouched, one finger over his lips. The dim streetlight filtered through the cracked boards, casting slices of gold across his face. His eyes had gone sharp, predator-focused, the softness from a moment ago gone like it never existed.

Then came the second sound—boots on gravel. Three sets. Maybe four.

They weren't in a hurry. That was worse. Scar's men didn't need to rush when they knew they already had you caged.

Colt moved without a whisper, sliding the shotgun into my hands. "Remember what I showed you," he mouthed. Then he drew both pistols, one in each hand, and slipped toward the stairwell.

My heartbeat thundered in my ears. The air smelled of rust, rain, and the faint burn of oil— familiar scents twisted into something terrifying in the dark. I crouched by the window, breathing slow like Colt taught me, praying my hands didn't betray the quake in my chest.

The first shadow appeared in the alley below—a tall man in a black hoodie, his face obscured. He signaled with two fingers, and more shapes emerged from the edges of the night, moving with the confidence of men who'd done this dance too many times.

A crackle of radio static drifted up through the boards. A voice, low and muffled:
"Target inside. Light it up."

My stomach knotted. They weren't here to scare us—they were here to erase us.

Then came the first explosion of sound.
The old metal door downstairs slammed open, hinges screaming, followed by the stomp of boots flooding

inside. Colt didn't wait—he fired first, the sharp crack of his pistol cutting through the night. A grunt, a crash, and then shouting.

I flinched as a bullet punched through the wood near my shoulder, splintering it like dry bone. Adrenaline burned away the fear, leaving only instinct. I rolled to the side, gripped the shotgun the way Colt showed me, and aimed toward the staircase.

Footsteps pounded up. Heavy. Fast.

I didn't hesitate. I pulled the trigger.

The shotgun kicked back, slamming into my shoulder as the blast lit the stairwell. A figure screamed, tumbling backward. The sound was raw and terrible, but I didn't let myself think about it. Thinking got you killed.

"Nay! Move!" Colt's voice ripped through the chaos.

I ducked and scrambled toward him, heart in my throat. He'd flipped over a metal worktable, using it as a shield, empty shells littering the floor around him. His teeth were clenched, eyes feral.

Three men surged through the stairwell—one limping, two unscathed. Colt took one down with a clean shot to the chest. The other two fanned out, firing. Bullets sparked against metal, ricocheting into shadows.

"Stay low!" Colt barked, shoving me flat as a spray of lead ripped through the boards behind us. Splinters rained down like hail.

I crawled to the duffel, fumbling for another shell, my fingers slick with sweat. One of Scar's men lunged around the worktable, knife in hand. He grabbed my arm before I could load, and instinct screamed louder than fear.

I bit him. Hard.

He howled, and I smashed my elbow into his throat. Colt was there in an instant, one arm snapping around the man's neck, twisting with brutal efficiency. The body dropped.

My stomach flipped, but there was no time to break.

"Window—go!" Colt ordered.

I grabbed the duffel, sprinting toward the boarded window on the far side. Colt fired behind me, covering the retreat. I slammed my shoulder into the boards until one broke free. Cold night air rushed in, carrying the metallic tang of the storm.

We clambered onto the fire escape just as another burst of gunfire erupted inside. Colt slid down first, pistol ready. I followed, my legs shaking but moving fast.

Halfway down, a figure emerged from the shadows—another of Scar's men, waiting. He raised his gun.

"Colt!" I screamed.

Colt spun and fired twice. The man dropped without a sound, his weapon clattering into a puddle.

We hit the alley and ran, rain splashing against our skin, hearts pounding in sync with the city's pulse. The Impala waited two blocks over, its dark frame blending into the wet night.

By the time we dove inside, our lungs were burning, clothes soaked, and my hands were still trembling around the shotgun. Colt started the engine, tires spitting water as we roared into the night.

He didn't speak until we were three streets away, the echo of gunfire fading behind us.

"That was Scar testing us," he said, voice low and ragged. "Next time, he's not sending boys. He's coming himself."

I swallowed hard, my pulse still wild. "Then we hit first."

He looked at me, and for a moment, his eyes softened again. "You're starting to sound like me."

"Maybe I'm finally learning how to survive like you."

The car sped deeper into the dark, and somewhere out there, I knew Scar was already planning the next move.

The Impala sliced through the wet streets, its tires hissing over puddles that reflected the bleeding neon of the city. My hands were still shaking around the shotgun, my body buzzing with the aftershock of adrenaline. Every heartbeat felt like it belonged to someone else.

Colt drove in silence, jaw tight, eyes cutting to the mirrors every few seconds. His shirt was damp with rain and someone else's blood. Mine too.

We had survived the ambush. Barely.

When he finally spoke, his voice was low, rough as sandpaper. "First rule of surviving Scar—never stay in one place long enough for him to catch his breath."

I nodded, staring at the streetlights blurring past. My reflection in the passenger window looked like a stranger—eyes wide, hair damp and wild, lips trembling even though I didn't feel cold.

"Second rule?" I asked, my voice barely above the hum of the engine.

"Hit back harder than he expects."

He said it like a promise, and the weight of it settled in my chest. For the first time, I realized we weren't just running anymore. We were circling back for blood.

He took a sharp turn down a narrow alley and killed the lights. The Impala coasted into a shadowed loading dock behind a shuttered warehouse. Colt shut off the engine, and for a moment, the world went quiet except for the rain and the tick of cooling metal.

I exhaled slowly, realizing I'd been holding my breath.

"Here," Colt said, handing me a rag to wipe my hands.

They were streaked with dirt and blood I didn't know if I wanted to scrub off or keep as a reminder. I cleaned them anyway, my fingers stiff.

Colt leaned back in his seat, head against the rest, eyes closed for a moment. He didn't look like a man resting—he looked like a man listening for death in the rain.

"Colt…" I hesitated. "Back there, I almost—"

He opened his eyes, fixing me with that predator's stare that could strip you bare. "Don't say it. You didn't. You're here. That's all that matters."

I nodded, chewing my lip. The air inside the car felt thick, heavy with what we weren't saying. The closeness of danger and the afterglow of survival left my pulse skittering in a way that wasn't entirely fear.

Colt leaned over suddenly, cupping my jaw in his calloused hand. His thumb brushed my lower lip, tracing the tremor there.

"You're shaking," he murmured.

"Maybe I like it," I whispered back.

The kiss wasn't soft. It wasn't tentative. It was heat and hunger and the violent relief of two people who should be dead but weren't. My hands gripped his shirt, feeling the flex of muscle beneath, the rapid thud of his heart matching mine.

He pulled me across the console, onto his lap, and for a moment, the world outside didn't exist. There was only the warmth of him, the rain pattering against the roof, and the wild, unspoken need to feel alive in a world that kept trying to bury us.

When his hands slid under my hoodie, I gasped against his mouth, every nerve alive. The intimacy was raw, electric, an unspoken pact between two broken edges fitting together.

But then he stopped, forehead pressed to mine, his breath ragged.

"We don't get to be careless," he said. "Not even with this."

I nodded, though my body screamed at the loss of him.

We shifted into strategy, though the heat between us still pulsed like a second heartbeat. Colt spread a rough map on the dashboard, marking Scar's territory with quick, precise strokes.

"Scar's gonna come harder next time," he said. "He's testing our edges, seeing where we break. We need to strike first."

"Where?" I asked, leaning over the map.

"He runs his cash and product through three main spots. The west side trap house, the midtown club, and the storage yard near the river."

"The club," I said immediately.

He arched a brow. "Why the club?"

"Because that's his ego. He owns the streets, but the club is where he flexes. You hit that, you hit his pride. He'll come bleeding for us."

Colt studied me, then nodded slowly. "You're learning."

"No," I corrected. "I'm leading."

He gave a low laugh, but there was respect in his eyes.

We spent the next hour mapping escape routes, identifying blind spots, and loading magazines in silence punctuated by occasional glances that said everything words couldn't. The rain tapered off outside, leaving the night damp and heavy, the city waiting for its next scream.

By the time Colt started the engine again, the plan was simple: move fast, hit hard, and don't miss.

I rested my hand on his thigh as he drove, feeling the tension coiled in his muscles.

"You ready for this?" I asked.

He glanced at me, his voice like steel. "I was born ready. Question is—are you?"

I met his gaze without flinching. "I'm not the same girl you picked up off that floor. I'm in this. All the way."

Jahari Hasahi Malik

The Impala roared back onto the street, and the city swallowed us whole.

Chapter 8 Velvet Knives and Red Lights

The club pulsed like a living thing.

Even from across the street, I could feel the bass vibrating through the wet concrete, the thrum of music mixing with the city's restless heartbeat. Neon lights bled across the sidewalk, catching in the puddles and broken glass like someone had spilled a bottle of liquid fire.

Scar's playground. His pride. His hunting ground.

Colt killed the Impala's lights a block away, letting the car disappear into the shadows of a graffiti-scarred alley. The rain had stopped, but the city still glistened as if it were sweating under its own heat.

"Last chance to back out," he said, his voice low, rough with the weight of what we were about to do.

I slid the small pistol into the holster he'd adjusted against my thigh. "Not a chance."

He gave me that look again—part admiration, part warning—before we stepped into the night together.

We walked like we belonged there, blending into the slow-moving line of partygoers waiting outside the club's steel double doors. The bass rattled my ribs, and the air smelled like spilled liquor, cigarette smoke, and heat.

A bouncer the size of a small tank scanned the line, eyes sharp despite the distraction of glittering dresses and high heels. His gaze lingered on Colt. Recognition flickered—faint, but dangerous.

Colt didn't flinch. He pulled me closer, his hand sliding over my hip in a move that was both protective and possessive. The heat of his touch grounded me, even as my stomach twisted with nerves.

When the bouncer waved us in, I exhaled silently. One obstacle down. A thousand to go.

Inside, the club swallowed us whole.

Red and purple lights cut through the dark, slicing across faces and catching the flash of sequins, diamonds, and too-white teeth. Sweat and perfume hung in the air, layered over the metallic tang of anticipation.

Scar's signature was everywhere.

On the high platform above the dance floor, his golden "S" insignia gleamed against a black wall. I could almost feel his presence, like a predator circling unseen.

"Remember," Colt murmured in my ear, his lips grazing my skin. "We're ghosts until we're fire. Don't draw attention."

"Then maybe don't touch me like that," I whispered, heat curling low in my stomach.

His mouth curved into a faint, wicked smile. "We need to sell the illusion."

"You're enjoying this."

"Maybe."

We moved through the crowd, weaving between swaying bodies and flashing lights. I let my fingers trail down Colt's arm, playing the part of the girl too drunk on love to notice the danger at her back. But my eyes were sharp, scanning for exits, for cameras, for the glint of weapons beneath jackets.

Colt leaned close, pointing subtly toward a side corridor. "Office is through there. Scar keeps his cash, ledgers, and maybe a few toys we can use."

We slipped off the dance floor, the music dulling to a muffled throb as the hallway swallowed us. It smelled of bleach and cigarettes, a stark contrast to the heat and glamour outside.

Halfway down, a locked door waited—black metal with a brass handle. Colt crouched, pulling a small set of tools from his jacket.

"You can pick locks?" I whispered.

He shot me a quick grin. "Baby, I've picked worse."

It took him less than thirty seconds. The door swung open, revealing Scar's private office: dim, sleek, and lethal. A desk with a leather top. Two monitors displaying camera feeds of the club. A safe against the far wall.

And a single red leather chair turned slightly toward us, empty.

Colt moved fast, rifling through drawers, shoving envelopes of cash into the duffel bag we'd carried in. I scanned the room, nerves buzzing.

Then something caught my eye—a silver lighter on the desk, engraved with Scar's initials. I pocketed it without thinking. Proof. A trophy. A reminder that we weren't just running anymore.

"Safe?" I asked.

"Working on it." Colt knelt by the heavy steel box, his fingers spinning the dial like he could hear its secrets.

That's when I heard it.

A laugh. Low. Cold. Close.

I froze, eyes darting to the doorway.

Scar stood there.

Tall, broad, wrapped in a dark suit that made the gold chain around his neck gleam like a trophy. His smile was sharp, his eyes colder than the steel he probably carried under that jacket.

"Well, well," he said, voice dripping with amusement and threat. "Look what crawled back into my house."

Colt didn't rise, didn't flinch. He just kept turning the dial, slow as sin. "You always were sentimental, Scar. Left your safe combination the same?"

Scar's grin widened. "I was hoping you'd be stupid enough to try this. Makes killing you personal."

His men appeared behind him, three shadows filling the hall. Guns glinted in the neon spill from the club.

Colt moved in a blur, yanking me down as Scar's first man fired. Bullets punched into the desk, splinters flying. I crawled behind the leather chair, heart hammering, ears ringing with the deafening music of chaos.

Colt returned fire, a clean, precise shot that dropped one man in the doorway. The others ducked, firing blind.

"Nay!" he shouted. "Cover me!"

I grabbed the pistol from my thigh, adrenaline surging like fire. I leaned around the chair and squeezed off two shots, forcing the second man back into the hallway.

Scar's laughter echoed over the gunfire, calm and cruel. "Cute. Real cute."

Colt lunged for the safe, twisting the handle. It swung open, revealing stacks of cash, a few pistols, and a black velvet bag. He shoved everything into the duffel, even as bullets shattered the glass of a wall frame behind him.

"Move!" he barked, grabbing my hand.

We sprinted for the window on the far side of the office, Colt firing once more to buy us a breath. His shoulder hit the glass hard enough to crack it, and rain-slick city air rushed in.

He shoved the duffel through, then me, before vaulting out himself. We landed on the narrow fire escape, metal groaning under our weight.

The city below yawned wide and wet and waiting.

And Scar's voice followed us into the night. "Run, lovers! I'll be seeing you soon."

The fire escape rattled beneath us as Colt led the way down, boots slick with rain. Every clang of metal against metal felt like it would echo across the whole city, alerting Scar that we were still breathing.

By the time we hit the alley, the club lights pulsed behind us like a heartbeat we had outpaced. My legs ached, my hands shook, and adrenaline still snapped through my veins like static.

Colt didn't stop until we reached the Impala, tucked deep in the shadows a block away. He popped the door, threw the duffel in the back seat, and slid into the driver's side. I sank into the passenger seat, chest heaving, body vibrating with leftover fear and thrill.

He didn't start the engine immediately. He just sat there, one hand on the wheel, one fist pressed against his thigh, breathing hard. Rainwater dripped down his jaw, catching in the stubble that shadowed his face.

"You good?" he asked finally, his voice rough, almost raw.

I nodded, but it was a lie. My whole body felt like glass, like one wrong move could shatter me into a thousand pieces. My pulse still raced, and behind it, heat coiled low in my stomach, twisting with the memory of his mouth on mine, his hands steady even in chaos.

"Lie better," he said, catching the tremor in my hands.

"I… I'm just—" I exhaled, staring at my lap. "I almost froze back there."

"You didn't. You acted. You're here. That's all that counts."

His voice was firm, grounding me, even as my heart tried to claw its way out of my chest. I turned to face him, and for a long moment, we just stared at each other. No city. No guns. No Scar. Just us in the hush of the rain.

Colt reached over slowly, his fingers threading through mine. "You did good, Nay."

The weight of his touch settled the shaking, just a little. I leaned into the seat, and the tension in my chest cracked open into something else.

Relief. Desire. Fear.

I wasn't sure which burned hotter.

When his hand slid up my arm, over my shoulder, and cupped the back of my neck, the answer didn't matter. I leaned into him, and the kiss was softer this time, slower, like we were both too aware of how close we'd come to losing it all.

The heat built anyway.

He tasted like rain and danger, and I melted into it, straddling his lap before I could think twice. His hands gripped my hips, grounding me as I pressed closer, needing the solid reality of him against me.

For a moment, I wasn't a girl with blood on her hands—I was just alive, every nerve awake, every beat of my heart synced with his.

"You drive me crazy," he murmured against my lips, voice rough with restraint.

"I thought you liked crazy," I whispered, tracing his jaw with my fingertips.

"I do," he said, hands sliding under the hem of my hoodie, heat blooming under his palms. "But this... This is different."

He kissed me again, harder this time, pulling me closer until there was no space left between us. The world narrowed to the smell of leather, gunpowder, and him.

When his lips trailed down my neck, a shiver ran through me, and my breath hitched. I could feel his heartbeat against my chest, fast and fierce, and for the first time in hours, maybe days, I felt safe—if only in this stolen, fragile moment.

Jahari Hasahi Malik

Then he stopped, forehead pressed to mine, and exhaled like he'd been holding the world on his shoulders.

"We can't stay here," he said.

I nodded, though every part of me wanted to pretend we could, just for one night.

Colt started the Impala, the engine's low growl vibrating under us. He drove slow at first, taking backstreets, letting the city fade from neon chaos to quiet, rain-slick emptiness.

Eventually, he pulled into a deserted auto garage, the kind of place that looked like it hadn't seen customers in a decade. He rolled the car into a shadowed corner and cut the engine.

"This'll do for a couple of hours," he said, glancing around. "Long enough to catch our breath before Scar's dogs sniff us out again."

I hugged my knees to my chest in the seat, exhaustion finally catching up to me. Colt reached back for the duffel, checking the haul. Cash. Weapons. A small velvet bag he hadn't opened yet.

He tossed me a bottle of water. "Drink. You'll crash harder if you don't."

I sipped, watching him in the dim light. Even when he wasn't looking at me, he was dangerous. Controlled. Beautiful in a way that made my chest ache.

"What's in the bag?" I asked softly.

He opened it and pulled out a gold-plated revolver, engraved with Scar's initials. It gleamed in the faint light, heavy with meaning.

"This," he said, spinning the cylinder slowly, "is Scar's ego in metal. He'll notice it's gone."

"So... now he's going to come for us?"

Colt smirked, but there was no humor in it. "Oh, he was always coming for us. This just makes it personal."

I reached across the console and touched his arm. He didn't pull away.

"Then we hit first," I said.

He looked at me, and for a heartbeat, the quiet stretched between us like a wire pulled tight— danger, desire, and something softer threading together.

"Yeah," he said finally, leaning back in the seat. "We hit first."

The garage had gone still, a cocoon of shadows and oil-stained concrete. I rested my head against the cool glass of the window, eyelids heavy. Colt had shifted into that alert kind of calm he wore like armor, one hand idly tracing the edge of the stolen revolver.

For a few minutes, it almost felt like the world had paused for us.

Then the world shattered.

A blinding flood of white light cut through the garage's cracked window, followed by the crunch of tires on gravel.

Colt's head snapped up. "We're burned."

I didn't have time to respond before the first bullet ripped through the garage door, showering sparks across the floor. The sharp tang of gunpowder hit my nose as instinct took over. Colt yanked me down onto the floorboards of the Impala, his body shielding mine as glass exploded above us.

"Move!" he barked, already shoving open the passenger door.

We rolled out onto the cold concrete, the Impala's frame groaning as more bullets tore into its side. My heart was a drum in my ears, every beat a countdown to death.

I crawled toward the nearest stack of old tires, Colt right behind me. More headlights flared outside the garage—two trucks, maybe three—boxing us in. The hum of engines and the shouts of Scar's men filled the night, a predator chorus.

"They found us fast," I whispered, breath shaking.

"Scar doesn't sleep when he's hunting," Colt said, voice flat, all steel. He peeked around the tires, counting heads. "Six men. Maybe seven."

"Against two."

A smirk tugged at his lips, dark and dangerous. "That's better odds than the club."

The first of Scar's men entered, boots echoing on the concrete. They fanned out, flashlights sweeping, guns raised.

Colt waited, coiled like a spring. When the closest beam of light hit the Impala's bullet-pocked door, he moved.

The gunshot was deafening in the enclosed space. The man dropped like a stone, and chaos erupted.

I squeezed the trigger on my pistol, my shot clipping the shoulder of a second intruder. He howled, firing back as Colt dragged me behind the next row of stacked tires.

Glass shattered. Sparks flew as bullets ricocheted off metal. The air smelled like smoke and fear.

"They're flanking!" I shouted.

"I see 'em!" Colt popped up long enough to fire two precise shots, dropping another man to the ground.

But the others kept coming.

A truck engine revved, and suddenly the garage door rattled hard before rolling up with a screech.

Scar himself stood framed in the blinding beams of headlights, his silhouette carved from menace. He didn't need to speak—I could feel his fury from across the concrete.

"Run all you want," he said, voice carrying over the gunfire. "You still die tonight."

Colt grabbed my hand. "Back!"

We sprinted deeper into the garage, weaving through shadows and rusted equipment. Another shot rang out, and sparks rained as a bullet kissed the steel beam inches from my head.

"This way!" Colt kicked open a side door, shoving me through into the alley beyond. Cold night air hit my face, carrying the smell of rain and exhaust.

We ran.

Feet pounding slick asphalt, lungs burning, hearts thundering. Behind us, Scar's men poured out, flashlights slicing the darkness.

Colt yanked me into a narrow cut between buildings, shoving over a trash bin to slow pursuit.

Jahari Hasahi Malik

The alley ended in a chain-link fence topped with barbed wire.

"Up!" he hissed.

He crouched, hands cupped, and I stepped into them, vaulting up the fence with adrenaline-fueled speed. Colt followed, grunting as he swung over just as a bullet clanged off the metal below.

We dropped into another alley, deeper in the city's veins now, and Colt didn't stop moving. His hand gripped mine, firm, unrelenting, until my chest ached from more than just running.

By the time we ducked into an abandoned laundromat two blocks away, my whole body trembled. Colt kicked the door shut behind us, and silence—fragile and trembling—settled like dust.

I pressed my back to the washing machine, chest heaving. Colt crouched in front of me, scanning my face, his own flushed with adrenaline.

"You okay?" he asked, hands brushing my arms, my waist, like he needed to feel I was really here.

I nodded, then collapsed into him, burying my face against his shoulder. He held me tight, his heartbeat a thunder I could feel through the soaked fabric of his shirt.

Scar had found us again.

And he wasn't stopping.

The abandoned laundromat smelled like rust, mildew, and old soap. Fluorescent lights flickered overhead, buzzing weakly as if even the bulbs were too tired to keep watch over us. I slid down against the cold steel of a washing machine, legs trembling from the sprint, chest aching from fear and adrenaline.

Colt crouched in front of me, his eyes sweeping over my face, hands skimming my shoulders and arms as if checking for bullet holes he might have missed in the chaos.

"You're sure you're not hit?" he asked, voice low but tight.

"I'm sure." My breath wavered. "You?"

He shook his head. "Not tonight."

For a moment, neither of us spoke. The city noise outside was distant, muffled by rain-slick walls and the broken door Colt had shoved closed. In this quiet, the reality of what had just happened pressed in like a vise.

Scar wasn't chasing us anymore.

Scar was hunting us.

I let my head fall back against the machine, eyes closing for a beat. "He's not going to stop, Colt. You know that."

"I know," he said, his voice heavier than I'd ever heard it. He ran a hand down his face, smearing rainwater and sweat. "We've been running on instinct. Jumping from shadow to shadow, hoping he misses. That ends tonight."

I opened my eyes, and he was looking at me—really looking at me—with that sharp, unflinching gaze that could strip away everything I tried to hide.

"So what?" I asked, though I already knew. "We run forever? Or... we finish it?"

Colt's jaw flexed. "We finish it."

He rose and began pacing the row of dusty machines, energy crackling off him like static. He looked like a man coiled around a storm—frustration, fury, and grim resolve all wrapped in one.

"Scar thinks he owns the streets," he said, more to himself than me. "Thinks he can drag us out of every hole we crawl into. He's not wrong—but he's got a blind spot."

"Which is?" I asked, wiping the sweat and rain from my forehead with my sleeve.

Colt turned toward me, and his eyes had that dangerous gleam I'd learned meant he'd already made the leap from survival to offense.

"He doesn't think anyone's stupid enough to come for him first."

I stood slowly, legs still shaky, and walked toward him. "You mean... we stop running."

"We stop hiding," he corrected. "We make him bleed in his own house until he knows he's prey, not a predator."

A shiver went down my spine, part fear, part thrill. This was the Colt who had been born in the streets, who didn't flinch from war when it knocked on his door. The Colt I'd kissed in the Impala, who made me feel like we were unstoppable—if only for the moments between heartbeats.

"You're serious," I said, my voice quiet but steady.

He closed the distance between us in two strides, his hand cupping my jaw. "I'm done letting him dictate when we die. If we're gonna take our shot, we take it now."

For a moment, the weight of his words—and the heat of his touch—sank into me. I could feel the pulse in his thumb against my skin, and the raw honesty in his gaze made my chest tighten.

"If we do this…" I swallowed. "We do it together."

Colt's mouth curved, not into a smile, but into something sharper—like agreement and promise all at once. "Always together."

The words sparked something electric between us, a slow-burning heat layered over the fear and exhaustion. Without thinking, I leaned in, our lips meeting in a kiss that was less about escape and more about claim.

It was slow, deliberate, a grounding reminder that we were alive, that we still had something to fight for. His hands traced my spine, pulling me closer, and I felt his breath tremble against my mouth.

"After tonight," he murmured against my lips, "we stop running. We take Scar off the board."

We spent the next hour in the dim laundromat, letting our heart rates settle while mapping out our next move with the quiet intensity of people who had no choice left but war.

Scar's club wasn't enough—he'd abandoned it the second we fled. He had other strongholds, other dens, but the one that mattered was his riverside warehouse. Colt knew it, and so did I.

"That's where he stacks his shipments," Colt said, drawing a rough map in the layer of dust on top of a dryer. "Weapons, cash, maybe product. He guards it like a dragon guards treasure. If we hit it…"

"He has to come to us," I finished.

Colt nodded. "And when he does, we end this."

The finality in his tone made my skin prickle. This wasn't a plan for a clean escape. This was a plan for war.

Outside, a siren wailed in the distance, bouncing off wet brick and glass. I leaned against the machine again, suddenly aware of how quiet it was now, how the world seemed to be holding its breath for what we were about to do.

Colt checked his weapons, his movements precise, methodical. When he looked up, his eyes met mine, and the unspoken question passed between us.

Are you ready to kill for this?

Are you ready to die for this?

I nodded.

Then he extended his hand, and I took it without hesitation.

We weren't running anymore.

We were loading the clip.

And Scar was going to feel every single bullet.

Chapter 9 Ashes and Aftershocks

Rain turned the riverfront into a silver blur, the kind of night where the city seemed to vanish under its own reflection. Scar's warehouse rose out of the mist like a shadow that didn't belong to anything human—hulking, black, and silent but alive with hidden eyes.

Colt cut the Impala's headlights a block away, coasting into an alley littered with broken pallets and weeds grown wild between the cracks. We sat there for a moment, the engine humming low, both of us breathing like we'd already run a mile.

"This is it," he said, voice steady, eyes scanning the structure. "No more running. No more waiting for him to find us first."

My fingers clenched around the pistol in my lap. Even in the dim light, I could see the taut lines of Colt's jaw, the storm just under his skin. He'd dressed in black from head to toe—hoodie, gloves, the faint glint of a knife strapped to his thigh. He looked like vengeance, like a man carved out of midnight and rage.

"You ready?" he asked.

I swallowed hard and nodded. "Ready."

The warehouse was guarded, of course. Two men on the loading dock, smoking under the overhang. Another pacing near the chain-link gate. Colt counted them with that quick, predator glance of his, then reached for the duffel.

We slipped out into the night, footsteps muted on the slick pavement. Rain slid down my hood, mingling with the sweat already prickling the back of my neck. My heart was a drumbeat, steady and loud.

When we reached the shadows beneath the loading dock, Colt pressed me against the wall with a gentle but firm hand.

"Wait for my signal," he whispered, his breath warm against my ear. "Two up top. I'll take left, you take right."

I nodded, nerves tightening into a coil in my chest. My body buzzed, a mixture of fear, adrenaline, and something else—something raw and electric that always came when Colt and I were on the edge together.

He moved first.

One moment he was crouched in the shadows, the next he was a blur of motion—silent, lethal. The guard on the left didn't even get to exhale his last drag before Colt's blade swept across his throat.

The other turned, eyes widening—then I squeezed the trigger. My shot cracked through the rain-soaked night, and he dropped like a marionette with cut strings.

Colt caught the body before it hit the ground hard, lowering it silently. He glanced back at me, that glint of pride in his eyes warming me in a way that shouldn't have felt good in a moment like this.

"Good," he mouthed.

We scaled the dock and slipped through a side door Colt had jimmied open with a thin piece of metal. The inside of the warehouse was a maze of shadows and steel—rows of crates, the faint hum of refrigeration units, and the drip of rain through a broken skylight.

Every nerve in my body was on high alert.

Colt moved like he belonged here, like he could see in the dark. He gestured for me to follow, and I did, heart pounding, trying to keep my breathing quiet.

We reached a corner stacked with crates marked with numbers and cryptic codes. Colt crouched, unzipping the duffel. He pulled out a small bundle of wires, tape, and two black cylinders.

Explosives.

"You weren't kidding," I whispered.

He shook his head, setting the first charge against the crate. "We take out his shipments; we take out his power. He'll come running."

The sound of footsteps broke the tension.

Two more of Scar's men entered from a far hallway, talking low, unaware of the bodies outside. Colt gestured for me to stay low, and we slipped behind another stack of crates.

The men's voices drifted closer—grumbling about the rain, about Scar's temper, about the whispers of the "ghosts" tearing through his territory.

Colt's hand found mine in the dark. His palm was warm, grounding. Our fingers laced tight, silent promise: together or not at all.

When the men passed our crate, Colt's arm flexed, and I knew the moment had come.

We struck as one.

He came around fast, his knife a flash of silver, and I fired twice, the muffled shots echoing like a heartbeat in the cavernous space. The men fell, and the warehouse swallowed the sound again.

We worked in tense rhythm, planting the other charges as the rain's drip became a clock ticking down. Every brush of Colt's hand against mine, every glance, carried weight—urgency, trust, and the unspoken question of how many more nights like this we'd get.

Finally, Colt whispered, "That's it. Time to leave a calling card."

He reached into the duffel and pulled out Scar's gold-plated revolver—the one we'd stolen from his club. He set it gently on a crate, in the beam of a flickering overhead light.

When Scar found it here, he'd know this wasn't random.

This was war.

Then the sound hit us.

Boots. Too many.

The main doors rattled as more of Scar's men stormed in, voices sharp, footsteps pounding on steel and concrete. They weren't whispering anymore.

"They found the bodies," I breathed.

"Then we're out of time," Colt said, grabbing my hand.

We sprinted toward the far exit, our footsteps splashing through puddles on the floor. A shout rang out behind us, followed by the roar of gunfire. Bullets sparked against steel as we dove behind a forklift, my heart hammering against my ribs.

"Go!" Colt urged, pulling me toward a stairwell that led to the catwalks.

We climbed fast, every clang of metal a beacon to the men below. Colt ducked low as a bullet tore through the railing beside him, showering us with rust.

We hit the upper level, weaving through shadows, and finally found the emergency door that led to a rusted fire escape. Colt shoved it open, rain and wind slamming into us.

He glanced back once, eyes dark and fierce. "Next part's yours, Nay. You ready?"

I gripped the railing, my pistol slick with rain, and nodded. "Let's burn his empire down."

The rain stung my face as we hit the fire escape, Colt's hand locked around mine like a lifeline. The metal groaned under our boots, slippery with moss and water. Every step rattled like it might give us away—or give out entirely.

Shouts erupted below, Scar's men spilling into the yard, flashlights and gun barrels cutting through the wet dark. The muzzle flare of the first shot lit the alley like lightning. A bullet pinged off the railing inches from my hand. I flinched but didn't let go.

"Keep moving!" Colt barked, his voice sharp, steady in a way that dragged me through the fear.

We reached the second landing, and he pushed me down behind the rusted railing, crouching low. I could feel the cold rain through my jeans, the vibration of the storm and our own ragged breaths. He pulled out the small black detonator from his hoodie pocket.

"Three," he said, his eyes meeting mine in the dark. "Two... one."

Jahari Hasahi Malik

He pressed the button.

The explosion ripped the night apart.

The first blast sent a shockwave through the metal under our feet, a thunderclap of fire and smoke that erupted from the loading bay below. The windows blew out in a chain of popping glass, and the interior ignited in a bloom of orange against the wet black sky.

I gasped, grabbing the railing to keep from tipping forward. Colt grabbed me by the back of my hoodie, dragging me down as a second blast shook the structure, heat rushing up even through the sheets of rain.

Scar's men screamed, some diving for cover, others firing blind toward the shadows where we'd vanished. The sound of shattering glass and twisting steel drowned out everything for a moment but the rush of adrenaline and the sharp scent of burning chemicals.

"We go now!" Colt yelled, pulling me to my feet.

We barreled down the last stretch of the fire escape, metal clanging beneath us. A third explosion hit—smaller, but close enough to make the staircase sway. Colt shoved me forward, and I jumped the final six feet into a puddle deep enough to splash my knees.

He landed beside me, grabbing my wrist before I could even regain balance. Smoke rolled over the yard, thick and black, and firelight flickered through it, turning the rain into a storm of gold sparks.

We sprinted toward the back alley, gunfire still chasing our heels. Shadows of men appeared through the smoke—coughing, shouting, some firing wildly. One figure emerged clearer than the rest, leveling his rifle toward me.

Colt moved without thinking, his shoulder slamming into mine as he pushed me behind a stack of wet pallets. He raised his pistol and fired twice—clean, efficient. The man dropped, his gun clattering on the slick concrete.

"You okay?" Colt asked, his hand brushing my cheek briefly before he scanned the yard.

I nodded, heart hammering so hard I felt it in my throat. "We need wheels, Colt. Now."

He tugged me along the narrow alley that snaked between the warehouse and the old railyard. The air was heavy with smoke and the metallic tang of rain and blood. My soaked hoodie clung to me, and every muscle in my legs screamed from the sprint, but I didn't stop.

Colt paused only long enough to yank a spare clip from his belt and swap out the empty mag. "We hit the side street, hijack something if we have to."

But Scar's men weren't done yet. A black SUV screeched around the corner, headlights slicing the smoke like knives. Its tires skidded on wet asphalt, and two men leaned out the windows with pistols raised.

"Down!" Colt roared, pulling me to the ground as the first shots rang out. Sparks flew from the brick wall inches from my head.

I rolled, scrambling behind an overturned dumpster, Colt's body covering mine for an instant that was both terrifying and intimate. His weight pressed me into the cold, wet concrete, the air thick with gunpowder and rain.

"You trust me?" he panted against my ear.

"Do I have a choice?" I shot back, voice trembling.

His grin was sharp and fast. "Then move when I move."

The SUV slowed, men shouting, guns flashing in the storm. Colt used the chaos as cover. He yanked a bottle from the duffel still slung across his back, the rag in its mouth already soaked in gasoline. I realized too late what he was about to do.

He lit the rag with a battered old lighter, eyes glinting with grim satisfaction, and lobbed the Molotov in a perfect arc. It shattered against the SUV's hood, fire blooming instantly, feeding on the rain-slick surface like it had been waiting for this moment.

The driver panicked. Tires screamed as the vehicle swerved, smashing into the corner of the warehouse with a sickening crunch. Flames licked up the windshield, and the shouts of the men inside turned to screams.

Colt didn't wait to see if they made it out. He pulled me up, and we ran, feet pounding against slick asphalt, adrenaline numbing the ache in my legs.

We finally reached the back street, the city opening up again in a wash of neon and rain. The Impala waited where we'd left it, crouched low in the alley, as loyal and dark as Colt himself.

He threw the duffel in the backseat and shoved me toward the passenger door. I slid in, wet clothes squeaking against the leather. Colt started the engine, the deep growl vibrating under my spine.

As we peeled out, I looked back just in time to see the warehouse fully catch, flames devouring Scar's empire piece by piece. The smoke rose thick against the night, a signal fire that would carry our names straight into Scar's rage.

"Tell me we hurt him," I whispered, almost to myself.

Colt's hand tightened on the wheel, eyes locked on the road ahead. "We hurt him. But we didn't finish him."

His gaze flicked to mine, and for a brief moment, the fire reflected in his eyes. "That comes next."

The Impala's engine purred low as Colt guided it into a forgotten stretch of the city, a place where streetlights flickered half-dead and graffiti claimed every wall like scars. Rain still traced silver rivers down the windshield, and the smell of smoke clung to our clothes, stubborn and heavy.

I leaned back in the seat, pulse slowly unclenching after the chaos of the warehouse. My fingers still tingled from gripping the pistol too hard.

"You good?" Colt asked finally, his voice soft in the dim glow of the dashboard lights.

I nodded, though my body told another story—every nerve wired tight, every inhale shallow. "I'm alive," I said. "That's… something."

He glanced at me, and for a second, the edges of his hard expression softened. "You were more than alive back there. You were… perfect."

A shaky laugh slipped out of me. "You mean shooting your way through hell is your idea of a compliment?"

"Only when it's deserved," he said.

He turned down an alley barely wide enough for the car, tires crunching over broken glass and loose gravel. At the end sat an abandoned garage, its sliding metal door rusted and tagged. Colt pulled a remote from the visor and pressed it; the door groaned open just enough to swallow the car.

Inside, it smelled of oil, damp concrete, and the faint sweetness of something left to rot long ago. But it was dry, hidden. Safe enough for now.

The engine cut off, leaving only the drip of rain from the eaves and the pounding of my heart in the silence. Colt leaned back against the headrest, eyes closed for a long beat, chest rising and falling like he'd been holding his breath the whole drive.

When he looked at me again, there was something raw in his gaze—equal parts relief and hunger.

He reached over, brushing wet hair from my face, his thumb lingering against my cheek. "You keep doing this to me," he murmured.

I swallowed, my own pulse stuttering. "Doing what?"

"Making me forget how much I hate this life… just by sitting here, looking at me like that."

The air between us thickened, humid with sweat and rain and adrenaline that hadn't yet burned off. My hand moved on its own, tracing the line of his jaw, rough from hours of stubble.

He caught my wrist gently, leaning into my touch, then guided my hand down to his chest where his heart thundered under soaked cotton. "Feel that?" he whispered.

I nodded.

"That's all yours. And it scares the hell out of me."

The kiss wasn't slow—it was a spark finally hitting gasoline. His mouth claimed mine with a heat that chased the chill from my soaked clothes, his hand cupping the back of my neck, pulling me closer. I slid across the seat without thinking, straddling him, the cold leather squeaking under us.

His hands gripped my hips, firm, anchoring me in a world that kept trying to swallow us whole. My hoodie clung to me, dripping, and he pushed it up just enough to feel the warmth of his hands against my skin.

For a moment, it wasn't about survival or vengeance—it was about now. About the pulse in my throat, the rough brush of his stubble against my jaw, the deep groan in his chest when my fingers tangled in his hair.

We broke apart only when breath became a necessity, our foreheads pressed together, his hands still holding me like letting go wasn't an option.

"This can't make me weak," he said finally, voice rough.

"It doesn't," I murmured, resting my head against his shoulder. "It makes you human. And right now, I need the human more than the gun."

101

He kissed the top of my head, a rare gentleness softening the edges of him. "Then the human's yours. But we can't stay here long."

I nodded, forcing myself to focus. "Scar's not gonna lick his wounds. He's coming hard, and he knows the city better than we do."

"Yeah," Colt said, finally leaning back. "He'll send every soldier he has. He can't afford to look weak."

"So what's our next move?"

He reached into the backseat and dragged the duffel into his lap, unzipping it to reveal the contents: two pistols, extra magazines, a short-barrel shotgun, and a scattering of cash and burner phones. He pulled one of the phones out, turned it on, and handed it to me.

"We need to make a call. Not to the cops— they're already half in Scar's pocket—but to someone who hates him enough to take a risk."

"Who?"

"An old contact. Runs guns for the East River crews. If we can arm up, maybe even trade him intel on Scar's weak spots, we get an edge before Scar pins us down."

I stared at the phone in my hand. "You trust him?"

Colt's eyes met mine, and his jaw flexed. "I don't trust anyone. But right now, I trust that Scar's gonna kill us if we don't move first."

I dialed, heart tight, listening to the rings echo in the dark garage. A gruff voice finally answered, suspicious, alert. Colt leaned in, speaking low but firm.

"We need guns, and we've got cash. Tonight."

There was a pause on the other end, and I swear I could hear the man's smirk in his voice. "If you're calling me, you're already in deep. You got two hours. Dock 14. Don't be late."

The line went dead.

I looked at Colt. "Two hours."

He nodded. "Then we plan. We stock up. And we finish this before Scar can corner us again."

I leaned into him for one last moment, breathing in smoke, steel, and rain. For all the chaos outside, here—just for a heartbeat—we were whole.

The garage felt like a held breath. Rain drummed a muted rhythm on the tin roof while Colt spread a city map across the hood of the Impala, wet sleeves rolled up. I traced the lines with my finger, following streets I didn't know by heart, trying to imagine our escape routes and how far Scar's reach could stretch.

"This is the last calm we're gonna get," he muttered, circling the docks with a sharpie. "After tonight, it's either Scar or us."

I leaned against the car, arms crossed. "I don't want calm," I said, my voice surprising me. "I want this over."

Colt's gaze flicked up to me, soft and dark in the low light. "You're stronger than you think."

"I have to be. With you, I don't get to be anything else."

He gave a quiet laugh, then looked back at the map. "We'll hit Dock 14, load up, then we move on Scar before he can regroup. If we—"

A sudden noise cut him off—**the crunch of tires on wet gravel outside.**

We froze.

Colt's head snapped toward the faint sliver of light under the garage door. Shadows moved outside, distorted by the rain.

"They found us," he said under his breath.

My pulse spiked, adrenaline surging all over again. Colt grabbed the duffel, slinging it over his shoulder, and gestured for me to stay low.

A metallic **clang** echoed through the garage as something hit the outer wall. Then a voice, muffled but sharp:

"COLT! COME OUT, AND MAYBE WE'LL LET HER WALK!"

I felt my stomach twist into ice. Scar's men weren't just here—they were playing with us.

Colt's jaw locked. "They won't let you walk," he whispered. "They'll drag you to Scar just to watch me break."

He handed me a pistol, meeting my eyes. "Stay behind me. If it goes bad, run through the side door and don't stop until you hit the street."

"I'm not leaving you," I hissed.

"You will if I tell you to," he said, voice low, fierce.

The garage door rattled as a crowbar wedged into its frame, screeching metal. Rain blew in through the gaps as the intruders pried it higher. Colt crouched behind the Impala, motioning for me to do the same.

The first man ducked under the door—a hulking silhouette, water dripping off his jacket. Colt didn't hesitate. **One shot, center mass.** The man crumpled silently to the concrete.

But the others didn't flinch. Shadows swarmed, boots pounding the floor, gunfire lighting the garage in staccato bursts.

I fired blindly, the recoil jarring my arms, sparks flashing as bullets chewed up the metal walls. Colt moved like a shadow, low and lethal, ducking between the car and the pillars.

"Get to the side door!" he shouted.

I crawled along the wall, heart pounding in my throat, until I reached the exit. I cracked it open, rain rushing in—and that's when I saw **the second SUV sliding into the alley**, headlights off, soldiers spilling out.

"They've got us surrounded!" I yelled.

Colt cursed under his breath and vaulted over the hood of the Impala, grabbing the shotgun from the duffel mid-motion. He racked it with a single smooth pump, the sound echoing like a warning.

Two men charged him from the left; he spun, firing once—**boom**—a spray of fire and rain. The first man dropped instantly, the second stumbled back, screaming.

But the third man used the distraction to shove me against the wall, gun pressed to my ribs. His breath reeked of smoke and sweat.

"Pretty thing like you," he sneered. "Scar's gonna—"

I didn't let him finish. I jammed my elbow into his throat with everything I had. He choked, stumbling back, and I fired the pistol point-blank into his shoulder.

He hit the ground screaming. Colt was there a heartbeat later, finishing the job before pulling me behind the car.

"You okay?"

"I'm not breaking," I said, my hands shaking but steady enough to hold the gun.

A bullet shattered the Impala's side mirror, the ricochet ringing through the garage.

"We can't stay," Colt said, eyes scanning for exits. "They'll burn us out if they have to."

As if on cue, a bottle with a lit rag arced through the gap under the door, landing against the far wall. Flames leapt up, licking across the floor, feeding on the oil stains and debris.

Smoke began to coil, bitter and black.

Colt grabbed my hand. "We're going out the back, now!"

We sprinted, ducking low, the heat at our backs. Bullets tore through the metal around us, sparks flying like fireworks. Colt kicked open the back door, and we stumbled into the rain-slick alley.

The storm was our only cover now, and Scar's men were close—too close.

Colt dragged me against the wall, his breath ragged, eyes hard with decision. "No more running after this. We take the fight to him. Or we die trying."

I met his gaze, the fire reflecting in both our eyes. "Then let's make him bleed."

Chapter 10 Dock Yard Inferno–

The rain had slowed to a cold drizzle, but the city felt like it was sweating danger. Streetlights painted the wet asphalt in streaks of gold and red, and every shadow looked like it could hold a gunman. Colt drove with his jaw tight, but for the first time since the safehouse burned, it was **my plan** steering us.

"Take the next left," I said, voice steady despite the tremor in my chest.

He glanced at me. "You sure about this?"

"No," I admitted, folding the map and tucking it into the glovebox. "But Scar's expecting you to come at him like you always do—loud, direct, reckless. We can't play his game. We have to play mine."

Colt's hands tightened on the wheel, knuckles pale in the dim dashboard light. "And your game is…?"

"Hit him where it hurts. Fast. Surgical. Leave him bleeding before he knows where to swing back."

We'd spent the last hour moving like ghosts through back streets, doubling back to shake any tails. The duffel sat at my feet, heavy with the new hardware Colt scored from the East River contact— two more pistols, a short-barreled rifle, and enough ammo to start a small war.

The plan was simple in theory, suicidal in practice: **infiltrate Scar's secondary operation**, take out the muscle, burn his stash, and leave a message that his empire wasn't untouchable.

Jahari Hasahi Malik

"Scar's gonna feel this in his chest," I said, scanning the skyline as we neared the industrial zone. "And when he does, he's gonna make a mistake."

"You really believe that?" Colt asked, tone caught between admiration and worry.

I nodded. "I believe in pressure. Everybody breaks if you hit 'em right."

We parked three blocks out, under the dripping skeleton of an overpass. The warehouse we were after was just visible down the road, its corrugated metal walls tagged in neon graffiti, a crooked security light buzzing above a side entrance.

Colt killed the headlights, and for a moment, the only sounds were the distant hum of traffic and the steady drip of water off the bridge.

He turned toward me. "This isn't like running. Once we start this… there's no walking it back."

I met his gaze, heart steady. "I'm not here to walk anything back."

The quiet between us stretched, thick with understanding and unspoken heat. Then we moved.

We slipped through the night like shadows, cutting across a littered lot to the rear of the warehouse. My sneakers soaked through in seconds, the chill cutting to the bone. Colt crouched low by the chain-link fence, scanning for movement.

"There," I whispered, spotting the pattern of lights through the grimy windows—four guards, maybe five, on rotation inside.

Colt smirked faintly. "You've got eyes like a sniper."

"Eyes don't matter if we freeze here," I said, and started climbing the fence before I could think too hard.

By the time my feet hit the other side, Colt was there, his boots silent against the wet gravel. We hugged the wall, moving toward the back entrance.

The door was locked, but Colt produced a small pry bar from the duffel. He worked it quietly, glancing over his shoulder, until the metal gave with a soft screech.

Inside smelled like oil and damp wood, the kind of rot that seeped into your clothes. The hum of a generator vibrated through the floor, and the faint flicker of fluorescent lights cast long, broken shadows.

I led the way, pistol up, breath slow. Every sense felt sharpened, alive. The sound of boots on concrete somewhere above told me the guards were split between the upper catwalks and the floor.

"Two on the catwalk," I whispered.

Colt nodded. "I'll take left, you take right?"

I hesitated, then shook my head. "No. I'll take left. You're louder when you shoot—use it to pull the others down here if it goes bad."

He grinned like he couldn't decide whether to be proud or scared of me. "You're really running this, huh?"

"Somebody has to."

I climbed the narrow metal ladder to the catwalk, moving slow, keeping low. The metal creaked under my weight, but the storm outside masked the sound. One of Scar's men leaned against the railing, smoking, oblivious.

I raised the pistol, breath steady, and squeezed the trigger. The pop was muted by the rain and distance. He folded silently, dropping his cigarette into the shadows below.

The second guard turned, eyes wide. He opened his mouth to yell, but I was already on him, slamming the butt of the pistol into his temple. He crumpled without a word.

Down below, Colt gave a low whistle—our silent signal. I peered over the edge and saw two more men heading toward him, weapons half-raised, suspicious but not yet certain.

He waited until they were within six feet before striking—**two shots, clean and quick.** Both bodies hit the floor like thunder.

The warehouse was ours. For now.

We moved fast, sweeping the interior. Crates stacked against the walls were stamped with false shipping labels—Scar's smuggling front in plain sight. I yanked one open and stared at the stacks of bills, bricks of uncut product, and a duffel stuffed with black-market pistols.

Colt whistled low. "Scar's not gonna sleep tonight."

"Good," I said, grabbing the gas can he'd brought. "Because neither are we."

We drenched the stacks, the smell of fuel sharp in the damp air. My hands shook with something between fear and thrill as Colt flicked his lighter, the flame catching in his dark eyes.

"You ready to start this war for real?" he asked.

I met his gaze, pulse loud in my ears. "I already did."

He tossed the lighter, and the fire bloomed, hungry and fast.

The flames reflected in the wet floor, lighting up the warehouse like a cathedral to vengeance. Sirens began to wail in the distance, faint but growing.

I grabbed Colt's hand. "Time to move."

We sprinted through the smoke, back into the night. The city swallowed us, but the fire behind us roared like a promise:

This wasn't running anymore. This was war.

We didn't speak for the first ten minutes after leaving the burning warehouse behind. Colt drove like the devil was in the rearview mirror, tires whispering across wet pavement, city lights flashing like gunfire on the windshield. My chest rose and fell too fast, and every breath felt like smoke.

The silence wasn't empty. It was heavy— charged with adrenaline, heat, and the thrill of surviving something we weren't supposed to. I watched Colt's hands on the wheel, steady and sure, his veins standing out against the faint glow from the dashboard. His jaw was tight, a muscle ticking like he was chewing down the part of him that wanted to let go.

"Breathe," he said finally, voice low and rough.

"I am breathing."

"Then slower. Or you're gonna black out on me."

I forced air in and out, counting like I used to in the pool during swim meets, when the water pressed in all around and the world above didn't exist. Slowly, the chaos in my chest settled into something sharper, quieter—and more dangerous.

We ducked off the main roads, cutting through an abandoned industrial park where shadows swallowed the streetlamps whole. The rain had eased into a drizzle, coating everything in silver. Colt pulled into a half-collapsed garage and killed the engine, letting the quiet settle like a dare.

I could still taste smoke on my tongue. My pulse was still sprinting.

Colt turned toward me. His eyes in the dark were molten, and I knew that look—it was the same one he'd given me in the safehouse, right before the world outside took everything from us again.

"Are you scared?" he asked.

"Only of stopping," I said honestly.

His hand slid to my jaw, his thumb tracing my cheekbone. I leaned into the touch like I'd been waiting all night, all week, my whole life. The world outside was fire and bullets, but in here... it was just us.

He leaned closer, his breath warm against my ear, and whispered, "You ran point tonight. You're the reason we're still alive."

The praise hit like a spark to dry wood. I grabbed his collar and kissed him hard, the taste of rain and gasoline still clinging to us. Colt groaned low, like he'd been holding back for hours, and pulled me into his lap. The Impala's worn leather creaked under us, but the car was our shelter, our universe in that heartbeat.

His hands roamed my back, urgent but careful, as if I might break under the weight of everything we'd survived. I kissed him again, slower this time, savoring the heat building in my chest, the grounding ache of being alive and wanting.

"We don't get many moments like this," he murmured against my lips.

"Then don't waste it talking," I whispered back, and he swallowed the words with another kiss.

For a few stolen minutes, the war outside didn't matter. There was only the hum of our bodies, the way my pulse matched his, the wet press of clothes and the slick heat of skin against skin in the dim light.

The world came crashing back with the sudden **flash of headlights across the broken windows.**

We froze.

Colt's arms tightened around me, eyes narrowing. "They found us."

My heart plummeted, the taste of him still on my lips as adrenaline tore through the haze. He set me gently back in the passenger seat and reached for the duffel.

The headlights slowed, then stopped across the street. Doors opened. Shadows spilled into the rain.

Colt's voice was low, steady, lethal. "Stay down. And remember… if they take me, you run."

I gripped my pistol and shook my head. "I'm not leaving you again."

Jahari Hasahi Malik

The sound of boots splashing in puddles filled the night. The stolen heat between us hardened into steel. We were done running.

The first boot splashed in the puddle outside the garage, and every instinct in me snapped taut. Colt's hand shot up, palm flat, signaling me to stay silent. The air between us felt electric, tight enough to hum.

The silhouettes moved through the rain like wraiths, their shadows stretching against the fractured walls. Three, maybe four men—hard to tell with the stuttering streetlight outside. Their muffled voices bounced off the concrete, low and sharp, all business.

"They split up," Colt mouthed.

I nodded, fingers curled around the pistol in my lap, my back pressed against the cold leather seat. My chest was tight with a mix of adrenaline and aftershocks from what we'd just shared in the quiet moments before danger found us again.

A beam of light cut across the garage, slicing through the slats in the boarded-up window. My breath froze in my throat. Colt shifted low, his body a shield between me and the threat. The light paused, then moved on, skimming over the wrecked shell of a van parked across the street.

"They're searching," I whispered, barely audible.

"They're hunting," Colt corrected, voice dark. "Big difference."

He reached over and squeezed my knee, grounding me in the shadows. Then he was moving, slipping from the driver's side door and crouching low behind the Impala. I followed, every nerve screaming, the wet gravel cold under my palms as I crawled after him.

The night swallowed us as we slid through a gap in the broken fence behind the garage, boots landing silently in the weeds beyond. The industrial park stretched ahead—rows of crumbling warehouses, rusting shipping containers, and pools of dirty rainwater reflecting the yellow glow of a single flickering light.

We moved in silence, becoming shadows ourselves. Every sound seemed amplified: the drip of water off the eaves, the distant echo of traffic on the highway, and the faint creak of a door somewhere behind us. My senses sharpened, and a strange calm settled in my chest.

Then—**a sudden metallic clang** shattered the stillness. I spun, pistol raised, heart leaping to my throat. One of Scar's men had kicked over a loose oil drum, and the sound echoed through the yard like a gunshot.

"Back here!" a voice barked.

Shadows converged, flashlights sweeping violently.

"Go," Colt hissed, gripping my wrist and pulling me into a run.

We sprinted through the maze of containers, boots splashing in puddles, adrenaline burning hotter than the cold night air. My lungs ached, but I didn't dare slow down. The men shouted, their footsteps splintering the darkness behind us.

We cut left through an alley of stacked pallets, Colt yanking me into a crouch behind a rusted dumpster. He held a finger to his lips, chest rising and falling as he listened.

"They're close," I breathed.

"Too close," he whispered. "We need high ground or a bottleneck. Somewhere to flip the script before they herd us into a corner."

I scanned the alley. A metal staircase clung to the side of a crumbling factory, its bottom half twisted and bent but still climbable. Without waiting for his signal, I sprinted to it, grabbed the wet railing, and hauled myself up. Colt followed, his boots silent on the metal as we ascended into the shadows above the street.

From the second-floor landing, we crouched and peered down. The men fanned out below, sweeping their flashlights across the lot. The light beams danced across puddles, then froze on the dumpster we'd just abandoned.

"They were here," one growled.

Another voice, gruff and certain: "They're not leaving this park alive."

My breath fogged in the cold, heart pounding. Colt glanced at me, the faintest smirk tugging at his lips. The chase had flipped—now it was our turn to hunt.

We crawled along the landing, careful not to let the rusted grates betray us. Rain whispered against the roof as Colt reached the edge and peeked over. One of the men lagged behind the others, scanning a stack of pallets with his back half-turned.

Colt glanced at me, raised an eyebrow, and mouthed: *Yours.*

The word lit a fire in my chest. I lined up my shot, exhaled, and squeezed the trigger.

The muffled pop was swallowed by the night. The man crumpled like a marionette with its strings cut, and his flashlight clattered into a puddle.

"Move!" someone shouted.

Chaos erupted below, but Colt and I were already slipping into the shadows again, cat to their dog, ghosts in the steel and rain.

The hunt had only just begun.

A voice cut through the rain like a razor. "Enough!"

It wasn't loud, but it didn't need to be. It carried weight—the kind of weight that silenced men and made fear coil tight in your stomach. Colt and I froze on the landing, our eyes locking before we dared to look down.

Scar had arrived.

He emerged from the black SUV that rolled to a stop at the edge of the industrial yard, his presence sucking the air out of the night. He didn't need a weapon in his hand; the two men flanking him carried that message for him—tall, silent, and lethal, their coats dripping rain.

Scar was older than Colt but sharper, like he'd been cut from glass and anger. His dark trench coat swung as he walked, and the streetlight caught the silver streaks in his hair. The cold smile on his face was worse than any snarl—it was the look of a predator who knows the game is already his.

"Y'all playing tag in my city?" he said, his voice carrying even over the drizzle. "Making me chase ghosts in the rain?"

No one answered. The remaining foot soldiers tightened their grips on their weapons, eyes darting toward the shadows where their buddy had just dropped.

Scar stopped in the center of the lot, exactly where the flashlights converged. He held out his arms, palms open, like he was welcoming the night.

"Colt," he called, his voice smooth, mocking. "You out here turning love into war again?"

My breath caught. He **knew** we were here.

Colt crouched low, one hand tightening on my arm to keep me silent. His jaw was iron.

Scar tilted his head, scanning the rooftops and shadows. "I can smell desperation. I can smell fear. And I can smell her."

He meant me. My stomach twisted.

Colt's whisper was a thread of steel. "He wants you scared. He wants you to move."

"What if he's already got us boxed in?" I murmured.

"He doesn't. Not yet."

But even as he said it, Scar's men fanned out, forming a net that would close in a matter of minutes. The SUV's headlights threw our perch into thin relief—one wrong move, and we'd be outlined targets against the rusted metal walls.

Scar's voice softened, like he was sharing a secret.

"You think I don't know what it's like to want someone so bad you'll burn the city for them? I invented that. You're just imitating the king."

My hands trembled—not with fear, but with rage. He was playing with us, savoring the hunt.

Colt's eyes met mine. No words, just understanding: **It's now or never.**

We moved.

Colt kicked a loose pipe off the landing, the clang drawing every gun upward. Then we sprinted along the grate, rain-slick metal groaning under our boots.

"On the roof!" a man shouted.

Gunfire erupted, deafening in the confined space. Sparks leapt from the railing as bullets chewed through metal. I dove behind a rusted vent, heart hammering. Colt returned fire, two precise shots dropping a guard near the pallets below.

Scar didn't flinch. He simply raised one hand, and his men moved like chess pieces around the lot, cutting off every escape.

"You're running out of rooftops, Colt!" Scar called, almost amused. "And the girl—" His voice dipped, soft and poisonous. "She's already mine. She just don't know it yet."

I felt something in me snap. Before Colt could stop me, I rose from cover and fired at Scar. The shot went wide, shattering a streetlight and plunging the corner of the lot into darkness.

Scar's laughter rolled up to meet us, deep and cold. "Oh… she bites. I like that."

We bolted for the stairwell at the far end of the roof, sliding down the slick metal steps two at a time. The rain turned the descent into a deadly game, every step threatening to spill us onto the concrete below.

Colt hit the ground first, reaching up to steady me as I jumped the last four feet. He grabbed my hand and didn't let go as we sprinted into the maze of containers. Behind us, Scar's voice carried one last time, calm and certain.

"Run. Make it fun. But you're not leaving my city."

The words chased us into the night, heavy as a promise.

We didn't stop running until the SUV headlights were only a memory. We ducked into a collapsed stairwell behind a gutted textile plant, our chests heaving, rain dripping from our hair and clothes.

Colt pressed his forehead to mine, eyes burning. "He saw you. He wanted you to hear him. This isn't just about me anymore."

"I know," I whispered, my voice shaking as much from fury as fear. "And he's never getting me."

He kissed me like a vow, fierce and unyielding. But in the back of my mind, I knew Scar had already rewritten the rules of our war.

Chapter 11 Blood On the Water

The rain hadn't stopped, but it had softened to a steady drizzle, drumming against the skeletal remains of the abandoned textile plant. We crouched under a broken awning, the concrete cold and wet beneath us, trying to catch our breath. My hair clung to my face, and Colt's knuckles were raw, smeared with blood that wasn't all his.

The city felt alive around us—breathing, watching. Every distant siren and echo of footsteps was a reminder that Scar's reach spread farther than we'd ever accounted for.

"This ends tonight," Colt said, voice low but certain. He was squatting on his heels, arms braced on his knees, staring at the puddle between his boots like he could see the entire war reflected in its ripples.

I didn't answer right away. I was still thinking about Scar's voice in the rain, the way it had curled around my name without even saying it. Like he was already inside my head, in our lives. My pulse quickened with anger, and the faint sting of fear mixed with something sharper: defiance.

"Yes," I finally said. "No more running."

Colt looked up at me then, and the intensity in his gaze made my stomach knot. He wasn't just planning an attack—he was preparing himself for the possibility that we wouldn't walk away.

We scavenged the Impala first, grabbing the duffel bags we'd stashed in the trunk before ditching it in the shadows. Inside were the tools we had left— two pistols, a shotgun, three spare clips, a combat knife, and the last three Molotovs we'd managed to scrape together before Scar's men burned our previous hideout.

I ran my fingers over the cold metal of the shotgun, the weight grounding me. "It's not enough."

"It's enough if we're smarter," Colt said, his voice flat with purpose. He slung the duffel over his shoulder and motioned for me to follow as we moved deeper into the plant.

The inside smelled like rust and rain-soaked wood. Old machinery sat frozen under decades of dust, and water dripped in rhythmic plinks from the broken ceiling. In the dim light filtering through the shattered windows, it almost felt like stepping into a cathedral for ghosts.

We set up in the manager's office, a crumbling box with a window overlooking the floor. Colt spread the weapons out across the warped desk, and I leaned against the wall, shivering in my damp clothes.

"What's the plan?" I asked.

Colt didn't look up as he loaded the shotgun. "We hit them before they hit us. Scar thinks he's in control. He thinks fear is enough to keep us reactive."

"And it isn't?" I asked, folding my arms.

His eyes finally met mine. "I'm done letting that man define the terms of our war. We go at him hard, we cut off his supply lines, and we smoke out his lieutenants. He's not untouchable—not if we start stripping away everything that makes him a king."

I thought about Scar's words, about how he'd said I was already his. A shiver crawled up my spine, but I forced it down and met Colt's determination with my own. "Then let's take his crown."

Before the night bled into morning, we mapped out the next moves on a piece of torn cardboard Colt found under a workbench. Three targets:

> **The North Dock**, where Scar's shipments came in under fake manifests.
>
> **The Glint**, a club that doubled as his command post.
>
> **The warehouse on Forty-Third**, where he funneled weapons and cash through a shell company.

"Hit the warehouse first," Colt said. "We cripple his operation from the ground up, and then we take the fight to his face."

I nodded, tracing a finger over the rough map. "And if he's waiting for us?"

"Then he bleeds first."

The quiet between us stretched, thick and full of unsaid things. The memory of our stolen moments in the Impala still lingered, a warmth that cut through the damp cold. I found myself watching the way the faint light caught on the edge of Colt's jaw, the small scar on his temple, the veins on his forearm as he prepped each weapon with careful precision.

I crossed the room, my boots echoing softly on the hollow floor. He didn't look up until I touched his shoulder.

"You know," I said softly, "if this is the last night we have… I don't want to waste any of it thinking about him."

His breath caught. Slowly, he set the shotgun aside and turned to face me. There was heat in his eyes again—controlled but undeniable. "Then don't," he murmured.

The kiss was slow this time, deliberate. It wasn't about running from death or claiming life in the middle of chaos—it was about *us*, about choosing each other in a world that was doing everything it could to tear us apart.

I could feel his heart pounding through his soaked shirt as he pressed me against the wall, the taste of rain and salt on his lips, the faint scrape of stubble against my skin. For a moment, the outside world ceased to exist.

When we finally pulled apart, breathless, I whispered, "Let's end this."

Colt's smirk was dark and full of promise. "We will. Together."

We moved out before dawn, silent shadows slipping into the city's veins. Scar thought he owned the night, but tonight, it was ours.

Scar liked the city best in the early hours, when the streets were slick and quiet, when the light was gray and soft enough to turn steel into silver. It was the hour before the world remembered to be alive—and the hour when he owned it the most.

He stood in the top-floor office of the Glint, his club, one hand resting lightly on the glass window that overlooked the empty dance floor below. The strobe lights were still, the bar wiped down to a shine, and the scent of last night's whiskey lingered faintly in the air.

Behind him, his men moved quietly, checking weapons, reporting on shifts, organizing crates. Scar barely listened. His eyes were on the city, where rain-specked streets reflected the glow of streetlights like fractured mirrors. Somewhere out there, Colt and the girl were breathing his air, running through his shadows, thinking they still had a chance.

They didn't.

"You hear anything?" Scar asked without turning.

Tino, still bandaged from his near escape, shifted his weight. "They hit the yard and vanished. I got three dead, one missing. They're ghosts."

Scar's jaw flexed. "Ghosts don't bleed, and I smelled their fear in the rain. Fear leaves a trail."

He turned then, his trench coat whispering against the polished floor. Tino avoided his gaze. The other men didn't. They knew better.

"Colt's smart," Scar said, voice low and deliberate. "Smarter than the average fool who thinks he can carve up my city. But smart doesn't win against me. Smart gets cocky, and cocky gets sloppy."

Tino swallowed. "What about the girl?"

Scar smiled faintly, the expression slow and cruel. "She's not a what. She's a *why*. That's how you break a man like Colt—cut his reason out from under him."

He moved across the room to the desk where a black ledger lay open, pages covered in his precise handwriting. It was more than numbers and names— it was the pulse of the city. Every backdoor deal, every bribe, every debt paid in blood or cash. Scar ran his finger down the page until he reached a single entry circled in red: **North Dock, 2:45 AM.**

"They'll hit the warehouse next," he said.

One of the lieutenants, a heavyset man named Brody, frowned. "You sure? They've been running for hours. Might lay low."

Scar turned his gaze on him, and the room went still. "Colt's pride won't let him. He's like me— when you back him into a corner, he bites. And he bites where it hurts most. He thinks I don't know my own reflection."

Brody nodded quickly, looking away.

Scar closed the ledger, the snap of the cover loud in the quiet office. "Set the trap. I want men on the roof, the alley, and both entrances. Nobody shoots until I say. I want him to *see* me before he dies."

The men dispersed, and Scar descended the stairs alone, moving through the empty club with the ease of someone who owned more than walls—he owned the heartbeat of this place. He could almost hear it now, under the hum of refrigeration units and the drip of rain through a crack in the ceiling.

He reached the back room where crates were stacked waist-high: weapons, cash, and black-market tech, all wrapped in plastic against the damp. Scar brushed his fingers over a box of handguns, as if they were old friends.

Colt's out there with scraps, he thought, a smile curling his lips. *And I'm the one writing the last page of his story.*

But even kings felt the weight of their crowns. Scar paused at the doorway, alone for the first time in hours, and lit a cigarette. The flame briefly illuminated the faint scar along his jaw—an old reminder that even predators bled if they weren't careful.

He exhaled smoke toward the ceiling and let the quiet settle.

Colt wasn't just another rival; he was a mirror Scar had thought he'd shattered years ago. The boy had run these streets in his shadow, learned the same lessons in blood and betrayal. Scar had let him live once, and maybe that was the mistake that would haunt him—or maybe tonight he'd finally close the book.

Either way, the city was his.

In another part of the city, the trap was already tightening. Scar's men were in position around the Forty-Third Street warehouse—perched on rooftops, crouched behind dumpsters, and waiting in unmarked vans that blended into the skeletal landscape of shuttered factories and chain-link fences.

A generator hummed softly in the alley, keeping the single flickering light above the loading dock alive. It illuminated just enough of the wet concrete to bait a trap, a perfect little stage for violence.

Scar would wait there himself, in the shadows, until Colt and the girl took the bait.
And when they did, the city would taste blood again.

The warehouse breathed with the city's pulse—slow, heavy, waiting. Scar crouched behind a stack of crates near the center of the floor, the air thick with the scent of oil and damp wood. The rain outside drummed against the corrugated roof in a steady rhythm, like a countdown only he could hear.

He didn't move. He didn't need to.

Jahari Hasahi Malik

His men were ghosts in the dark, their positions memorized, their fingers steady on triggers. He'd arranged them like a symphony, every player in place to compose a single, violent crescendo. He could practically hear it: the echo of gunfire, the scream of splintered wood, the wet thud of lives ending.

"Check in," he murmured into the mic clipped to his collar.

One by one, the voices came back, low and tight:

"North roof—clear."

"South alley—clear."

"East van—ready."

"West stack—ready."

Scar closed his eyes for a moment and let the control wash over him. This was his art. Chaos in the streets, yes—but here, he was the conductor.

He thought of the girl, the fire in her eyes as she'd taken that reckless shot. It hadn't scared him—it had intrigued him. Desire and defiance were a dangerous mix, and Scar thrived on danger.

He could see her now in his mind's eye: damp hair clinging to her cheek, lips parted as she fought to keep her courage from slipping. Colt might have taught her how to run, but Scar was going to teach her something else entirely—how it felt when running wasn't enough.

He smirked, just a flicker of expression in the darkness.

A soft tap crackled in his earpiece—two clicks. The signal from the west stack.

"They're here," a whisper came through, almost reverent.

Scar's pulse didn't spike; it simply settled into that familiar predator's rhythm. He adjusted his stance, resting one hand lightly on the matte-black pistol at his hip.

"Positions," he said quietly.

The warehouse seemed to hold its breath.

Through the slit in the loading dock door, headlights flashed briefly as a vehicle crept past. It didn't stop. A beat later, movement flickered in the shadows near the north corner—a ghost slipping across the rain-slick concrete. Scar didn't need to see his face to know it was Colt.

"Hold," Scar murmured into the mic.

A rat scurried across the floor, its tiny claws skittering over metal. Scar's men stayed frozen, disciplined. That was why he trusted them.

He thought back to nights long ago when he'd been on the other side of this game. Young. Hungry. Believing the city was his to take, only to learn the hard way that it took you back. Colt reminded him of that version of himself—smart enough to be dangerous, too stubborn to quit.

The difference was Scar had learned to stop believing in mercy.

Footsteps. Soft, deliberate. Two sets.

Scar could almost feel the girl now, close enough to taste her fear in the damp air. He crouched lower, eyes trained on the narrow path between the crates that would lead them right into his teeth.

129

The first silhouette appeared—a flash of movement, dark against darker. Then another, smaller. Scar's mouth curled into that cold smile again.

Welcome to my house, he thought. *Let's see how long you last.*

He raised one hand, and every shadow in the warehouse seemed to lean toward him, waiting for the silent cue to pounce. But Scar didn't give it yet.

He wanted them to step closer. To *feel* the trap.

A whisper in his earpiece: "Take the shot?"

Scar's voice was a calm blade. "Not yet."

He watched as Colt guided Nay deeper into the kill zone, her head swiveling, shoulders tense, pistol clutched in both hands. Brave, but scared. He could smell it.

Colt paused near a stack of crates, scanning the room. He knew something was wrong. Scar could almost read the calculation in his stance—the slight crouch, the shift of weight, the way he pressed a hand lightly to Nay's hip to guide her behind cover.

Smart boy.

Scar almost respected him for it.

Almost.

"Close the doors," Scar said, quiet but lethal.

A metallic clang split the silence as the massive loading doors dropped from above, sealing with a shuddering echo. The sound made the girl jump, and Scar savored it.

Colt spun, gun raised, eyes narrowing in the dark. The flashlight he snapped on carved a sharp beam through the gloom, catching on metal, wire, and dust—but never on Scar.

Scar waited, a shadow among shadows, letting the tension coil tighter.

Then he finally spoke, his voice carrying through the cavernous space like the whisper of a blade unsheathing.

"Welcome home, Colt."

The echo of those words was better than gunfire. It was the sound of fear blooming in the dark.

The echo of Scar's voice curled through the warehouse like smoke, low and intimate, making every hair on my arms rise. My finger twitched against the trigger. Colt didn't move.

He knew better.

A single overhead light flickered to life with a metallic hum, illuminating a small circle of wet concrete near the center of the floor. The rest of the warehouse stayed drowned in darkness, broken only by faint shafts of moonlight through the high, cracked windows.

Scar was still invisible, but his presence filled the room like a second heartbeat.

"Drop the girl and maybe you walk," Scar's voice came again, smooth as oil, closer this time.

"Not happening," Colt said, his voice echoing hard against the steel and concrete.

I held my breath, pressed to the side of the crate, my heart thudding against my ribs. There was a strange, almost sacred stillness to it all—the way the rain softened on the roof, the way the city outside seemed to pause, waiting for who would bleed first.

Jahari Hasahi Malik

A slow, deliberate footstep echoed. Then another.

Scar emerged from the shadows, his black coat slick with rain, collar turned up. He walked into the faint pool of light like he owned it, his sharp jaw catching the glint for a second before the rest of him stayed hidden by the dark.

I had seen him before, but never like this. Up close, he radiated something beyond danger— *inevitability*.

"You've been busy," Scar said to Colt, as if they were old friends catching up. "I almost admired it. But then you made it personal."

Colt didn't flinch. He didn't raise his voice. "It's always been personal."

Scar's faint smile barely reached his eyes. "You stole from me. You killed my men. And you brought her into it." He tilted his head slightly toward me. "That's your weakness talking, not your brain. And you know how I deal with weakness."

The room was so quiet I could hear the slow drip of rainwater from the rafters.

Colt finally stepped forward, into the light. Water dripped from his hair onto his leather jacket, his pistol steady in his hand, his face carved from stone.

"You want her?" he said, voice low but steady. "You'll have to take me first."

Scar's laugh was soft, almost a purr. "That was always the plan."

Another set of footsteps shifted in the shadows. I tensed, my gaze darting to the corners of the warehouse. There were eyes everywhere. Shapes in the dark. Guns in the gloom.

Scar raised a hand, and the shadows stilled like obedient dogs.

"You think you're the first to challenge me, Colt?" Scar's voice hardened now, a predator's growl beneath the smoothness. "I built this city from bones. I buried men deeper than you, and the streets forgot them before the rain even dried."

"Then bury me," Colt said, "but I'm taking your crown with me."

Scar studied him for a moment. The silence was unbearable, thick with the weight of everything unsaid: the history between them, the blood already spilled, the lives hanging on what came next.

Then Scar's eyes slid to me, dark and deliberate.

"You," he said softly, and the sound of it made my stomach clench. "Do you really know what he is? What he's done? Or are you just holding onto a dream you can't afford to keep?"

I felt heat rise to my face, anger coiling in my gut. "I know enough," I said, voice steady, even though my heart was pounding.

Scar smiled, slow and dangerous. "Good. That means you understand the price."

Colt stepped in front of me slightly, a subtle shield, and the sight of it made my chest ache. For a heartbeat, the world shrank to just the three of us, bathed in the dim circle of light while the city's underworld waited, silent and hungry, for the first crack of thunder.

Scar's hand moved, brushing back his coat to reveal the matte black pistol at his side.

"Last chance," he said, his voice a quiet blade. "Walk away, Colt. Leave her here, and maybe I let you crawl out of my city alive."

Colt's answer was a sharp exhale, almost a laugh. "You talk too much."

Scar's eyes lit with something electric— anticipation, maybe even respect. His hand twitched.

And in that suspended second, the warehouse *exhaled*.

Men shifted in the shadows, muzzles catching the faint light. My heart hammered as Colt's hand squeezed mine for a split second, a silent *get ready*.

The city's pulse seemed to sync with mine as I took aim, my breath held.

Then Scar whispered, almost reverent: "Alright. Let's dance."

The first gunshot cracked like a shattering world.

Chapter 12 Safe Houses and Dangerous Hearts

The warehouse erupted into a thunder of gunfire.

I dove behind a stack of crates with Colt, the splintering wood raining over us as bullets shredded the air. My ears rang with the sound—each shot a metallic scream against the corrugated steel walls, every muzzle flash like a strobe of chaos.

"Stay low!" Colt barked, yanking me closer to him as a round chewed through the crate inches from my head.

The air was thick with gunpowder and the sharp bite of adrenaline. My pulse pounded in my throat, so loud it almost drowned out the chaos. Almost.

From the catwalk above, Brody sighted down the barrel of his rifle, scanning for Colt in the dim light. He breathed through his teeth, steady and patient, waiting for the moment his boss's enemy exposed himself. Below him, shadows flitted—other men moving into positions, a pack of predators tightening the noose.

"Keep 'em pinned," Tino growled from the east stack, voice low in the comms. "Scar wants him to feel it first."

Bullets rained again, and sparks spat from a metal drum near the center of the floor.

Colt rose for a second, fired three shots, then ducked again. A grunt echoed from somewhere above, and I didn't know if we'd hit someone or just scared them.

"Two on the catwalk," Colt said, breathing hard, his voice all grit. "Another four on the ground. Maybe more."

"What about Scar?" I asked, whispering, clutching my pistol like it could anchor me.

Colt met my eyes briefly, a flash of intensity. "He's here. He always waits for the right moment."

I nodded, though fear coiled in my stomach. This was his world, not mine, and every second felt like a knife's edge.

Scar crouched in the shadow of the far wall, calm amid the storm he'd orchestrated. His gun was warm in his hand, but he didn't fire. Not yet. He wanted Colt cornered, broken, *aware*.

"Push them left," he ordered through the mic, voice smooth as glass. "I want him in the open."

Men moved like chess pieces, sliding from cover to cover. Two flanked along the rusted conveyor belts. Another crept behind a stack of crates near the west wall. Scar watched it all, the predator watching his prey get funneled into the kill zone.

Colt swore under his breath as another burst of bullets tore through our cover. One crate splintered in half, spilling dusty coils of rope across the floor.

"They're herding us," Colt muttered.

"Then what do we do?" I asked, my voice shaking despite myself.

He reached over, his hand gripping mine for a heartbeat—firm, grounding. "We don't play by their script."

He grabbed a metal pipe from the floor and flung it toward the opposite wall. The clang echoed like a gunshot, drawing a quick barrage of fire in the wrong direction.

"Move!" Colt hissed, and we scrambled to new cover, boots slipping on the slick concrete. My chest burned, but I didn't let go of the pistol.

Brody cursed. "They're shifting right—lost visual!"

"Keep the pressure," Scar said, voice calm but cutting.

Another man, crouched near the generator, caught sight of movement. "Got 'em. By the west wall—"

Colt's shot dropped him mid-sentence, his body crumpling into shadow.

The radio filled with brief static, then silence.

Scar's jaw tightened. He didn't flinch at death, but he noticed the pattern. Colt wasn't just running—he was *thinking*.

We slid behind another stack of crates, panting. Colt reloaded with fast, practiced movements. I tried to slow my breathing, but my chest heaved with adrenaline and terror.

"Are we gonna make it out?" I whispered.

Colt glanced at me, his expression unreadable but fierce. "We're gonna make them regret underestimating us."

His hand brushed my cheek for half a second, grounding me again. Then he leaned out and fired twice, the muzzle flash lighting his jaw like a promise of vengeance.

A scream echoed from somewhere high above. Another man down.

Scar finally moved, slipping from the shadows like a phantom. He stalked toward the center of the floor, boots silent on wet concrete.

He relished the dance—the rhythm of chaos bending to his will. But Colt was making it interesting, and that stoked the fire in his veins.

Through the flickering light, he saw a shadow move—Nay. Scar's lips curved in a cold smile.

He raised his pistol and spoke into the mic. "Close the trap. They don't leave this room breathing."

The warehouse had gone quiet for a moment.

Not silent—never silent—but the staccato of gunfire had faded, replaced by the distant drip of rain through the cracked roof and the soft hiss of steam rising from somewhere in the machinery.

Colt yanked me into a narrow alcove between two rusted support beams, his chest pressed against mine as we crouched low. My heart was racing, pounding so hard it felt like it might echo into the darkness and give us away.

"You okay?" he whispered, voice rough in my ear.

I nodded, but my hands trembled around the pistol. "I think so… yeah."

He studied me for a moment in the dim light, his eyes a dark, steady heat. Rainwater dripped from his hair onto his jaw, and his breathing was fast, but controlled. Somehow, in the middle of this hell, he still managed to look like the kind of man you could fall into and forget the world burning around you.

A soft groan echoed from across the warehouse, followed by the faint shuffle of boots. The enemy was repositioning, hunting.

I swallowed hard. "They're not giving up."

"They won't," he said. His hand slid along my arm, firm and grounding, before resting briefly at my waist. "But they'll make mistakes. Scar always pushes too hard in the end."

I knew we had seconds—maybe a minute—before we had to move again. But in that pocket of stillness, with the danger pressing in from all sides, the adrenaline shifted into something sharper, something hot and reckless.

"You're shaking," Colt said softly, his thumb brushing my hip through my damp shirt.

"I'm scared," I whispered, and then, quieter: "And... I'm not."

His brow furrowed in question, but before he could ask, I leaned up and kissed him—urgent, desperate, tasting of fear and rain.

Colt froze for a heartbeat, then pulled me closer, his mouth claiming mine like we had no promise of tomorrow. The weight of his body pressed against me, heat cutting through the chill of the warehouse, his hand sliding up my back, anchoring me in the chaos.

Every nerve was lit, alive with the twin currents of danger and desire. The world beyond our bodies—the guns, the shadows, Scar—faded into nothing for that single, stolen moment.

He broke the kiss first, forehead resting against mine, his breath ragged. "You pick the worst times to be irresistible, you know that?"

A trembling laugh escaped me, the sound half-hysterical. "Blame the adrenaline."

"Adrenaline's a liar," he murmured, but there was a flash of heat in his eyes that said he wasn't complaining.

The tension between us hummed, electric and raw, but reality snapped back in with a distant clatter of metal. Someone was getting closer.

Colt's hands flexed once on my waist before he pulled back, the soldier in him taking over again. "We move. Now."

We slipped out of the alcove and back into the shadows, boots silent on the damp concrete. Colt led, his body a moving shield, every step purposeful. I followed close, forcing my heartbeat to steady, forcing my fear to focus into something sharper—something useful.

We crept along the wall until we reached another stack of crates. Colt held up a hand, signaling me to stop. I crouched, clutching my pistol, while he leaned just enough to peek around the corner.

I caught a glimpse of his face in the dim light—calm, lethal, and mine for however long fate let me keep him.

A voice echoed from somewhere above. Scar's voice.

"You can't hide forever, Colt. This place is a grave, and you're already in it."

Colt's jaw tightened. He leaned back toward me, his lips brushing my ear. "We're going to turn his grave into his pyre."

I nodded, adrenaline surging again, the kiss still burning on my lips.

The warehouse was breathing.

That was the only way I could describe it— the creak of steel girders, the low moan of wind through broken windows, the faint drip-drip-drip of rainwater falling from the rafters. In the darkness, it felt alive, like the building itself was holding its breath, waiting to see who would die next.

Colt and I crouched behind the crates, and for a moment, the world shrank to the sound of my heartbeat, loud and frantic.

Then came the *other* sounds.

Boots.

Slow, deliberate, and wrong somehow. Not the rushed steps of a man running into battle—these were careful, stalking footsteps, circling us.

I gripped my pistol tighter. Colt motioned for silence, his eyes like flint in the dim light. He had gone completely still, every muscle coiled, listening.

Somewhere to the left, metal scraped against metal.

The sound was small, but in the cavernous warehouse, it echoed like a scream.

I clamped my teeth down on a gasp, my stomach knotting. Colt tilted his head, mapping the sound, his hand brushing mine for just a heartbeat—a silent reassurance.

Jahari Hasahi Malik

We were being hunted.

From the catwalk above, a shadow passed across one of the flickering lights. I froze, watching it move with a predator's patience.

Scar's men weren't rushing us now. They were enjoying this, dragging out the kill. Like wolves circling wounded prey.

Another step. Another drip of rain. A faint crunch of glass somewhere behind us.

It was like a horror film, every sound amplified until my pulse felt like it was going to explode in my throat.

I caught a whisper—actual words this time.

"...check the west side..."

The voice was low, maybe ten feet away, and it sent a cold ripple down my spine.

Colt leaned in close, his breath warm on my ear. "Two flanking. One on the catwalk. Another behind us."

He didn't need to say the next part: *They're tightening the noose.*

I nodded once, slow, every sense on fire.

The darkness pressed in closer, thick with danger. My palms were slick, the weight of the pistol suddenly immense. Every nerve screamed that we were seconds from being discovered, that the next flicker of light would give us away.

A sudden *clang* of metal echoed across the warehouse—something falling, or being kicked.

I jerked toward the sound, heart slamming against my ribs, but Colt didn't move. He stayed still as a shadow, eyes scanning.

Then, from the darkness, a low laugh floated through the air.

Scar.

"You feel that?" he called softly, his voice curling like smoke around us. "That's the city telling you it's over."

The footsteps grew louder.

Someone on the catwalk above us shifted, the wood creaking under his boots. Another man's shadow passed along the far wall. We were surrounded, the walls closing in, every breath feeling like it might be our last.

I pressed against Colt without thinking, his solid warmth the only thing holding the panic at bay.

He leaned in, lips near my ear, whispering: "On my mark, we break left. Shoot anything that moves."

I nodded, forcing my shaking hands to steady.

Then the first flashlight beam cut across the darkness.

I flinched as it passed just inches from our faces, sliding along the edge of the crate. We froze.

The beam moved on, slow, deliberate, sweeping like the eye of some hungry predator.

Every muscle in my body screamed to run, to shoot, to *do something*—but I stayed frozen, following Colt's lead, until the light disappeared again.

The silence that followed was unbearable.

143

Then Scar's voice came again, smooth and intimate, like he was standing right beside us.

"Time's up."

A single gunshot shattered the silence, and the world erupted again.

The single gunshot ripped through the warehouse, sparking chaos.

Screams and shouts followed, boots pounding on metal and concrete, shadows scattering like startled birds. Colt shoved me behind a stack of pallets as a second shot cracked the air, splinters exploding inches from my face.

Then, through the chaos, Scar appeared.

He moved like the storm belonged to him—slow, deliberate, untouchable. The dim light caught the lines of his face, sharp and wolfish, eyes lit with a predator's satisfaction. His coat hung heavy and wet against his frame, his gloved hand wrapped around a matte-black pistol.

"You made me work for this," Scar said, his voice low but carrying across the room. "Almost respect that."

Colt rose from behind cover, gun trained on Scar, his body tense with coiled fury. "Almost's all you'll ever get from me."

Scar chuckled, stepping closer, boots echoing in the cavernous space. Around us, his men held their positions, guns raised but not firing—this was Scar's show now.

"You should've stayed gone," Scar said, tilting his head, almost casual. "Could've lived whatever life you were pretending to have. But you came back. Dragged her into it."

His eyes slid to me, dark and assessing, and I felt the weight of his attention like a knife.

"She doesn't belong here," he said, and his voice softened in a way that was somehow worse than shouting. "She's just a body that bleeds for your mistakes."

"Say her name," Colt growled.

Scar's grin widened, cruel and taunting. "Nay."

Hearing my name in his mouth made my stomach twist, but I forced my spine straight, lifting the pistol with both hands.

"Talk all you want," I said, voice steady despite the tremor in my chest. "You're still dying tonight."

Scar's expression sharpened—pleased, maybe even amused.

"Fiery," he said, stepping closer. "I like that. Shame you're betting your life on him."

The tension snapped like a tripwire. Colt fired first.

Scar dove sideways with inhuman reflexes, the bullet ricocheting off metal. His men erupted into motion, and the warehouse became a blur of gunfire, shouting, and sparks.

I scrambled for cover as rounds chewed through the wooden pallets, Colt rolling to a better angle. Scar, crouched behind a steel beam, fired twice, forcing Colt back.

Then he moved again, closer, like a wolf stalking a cornered rival.

145

"Face me, Colt!" Scar's voice rose above the cacophony. "Let's end this without the noise."

Colt glanced at me once—quick, weighted—and then he was moving, circling toward Scar, sliding behind crates and machinery.

I followed, heart in my throat, staying low. Every nerve screamed that this was suicide, but there was no leaving him.

Finally, Colt and Scar collided in the open, just a few feet of slick concrete between them.

No more hiding.

Scar lunged first, a flash of movement, and Colt met him halfway. The guns were forgotten for a moment as fists and elbows became weapons.

Colt's punch cracked against Scar's jaw, but Scar twisted, catching him in the ribs with a brutal hook. They moved like predators, fast and savage, grunting with every impact.

I circled, trying to keep my pistol up without hitting Colt, but the fight was chaos, a tangle of motion and rage.

Scar grabbed Colt by the coat and slammed him into a rusted support beam, the clang echoing like a bell. Colt staggered, teeth bared, and slammed his forehead into Scar's face. Blood sprayed, and Scar staggered back, laughing.

"Finally!" he roared. "The man I wanted to kill!"

Colt surged forward, tackling him to the ground. They rolled through dirt and puddles, fists flying. Scar's knife flashed in the dim light, slicing

Colt's arm, but Colt didn't stop—he pinned Scar with raw strength, landing blow after blow.

I moved closer, my pistol trained, but my heart was in my throat.

"Colt!" I shouted. "Finish it!"

Scar spat blood, grinning up at us through split lips. "Do it. But if you don't kill me clean, I'll haunt you forever. Both of you."

The moment stretched, soaked in rain, blood, and the scent of gunpowder.

Colt pressed the barrel of his gun against Scar's forehead.

Scar went still.

For a heartbeat, the world was silent again, except for our ragged breathing.

Then the sound of approaching sirens shattered the spell.

Colt swore, eyes darting toward me. Scar's surviving men were already pulling back, fading into the shadows—they knew the police were close.

Scar laughed again, a broken, bloody sound.

"This isn't over," he rasped. "This is just the first chapter."

Colt hesitated for a fraction of a second too long.

Scar twisted suddenly, kicking Colt off him and disappearing into the maze of machinery. By the time Colt was on his feet, Scar was gone, leaving only the echo of his laugh and the promise of war.

I ran to Colt, adrenaline shaking me to my core. He grabbed my hand, pulling me toward the exit.

147

Jahari Hasahi Malik

"This city's about to burn," he said, voice ragged but certain. "And we're the ones holding the match."

Chapter 13 The Hunter's Hour

The motel smelled like old cigarettes and damp carpet.

Colt locked the door behind us and slid the chain into place before collapsing into the single armchair, his bloody arm hanging off the side. I dropped the duffel by the door and leaned against it, suddenly too exhausted to stand.

For a long moment, we didn't speak. The only sounds were the hum of the flickering fluorescent light and the distant rumble of traffic from the highway beyond the paper-thin walls.

When I finally pushed away from the door, my legs felt like they didn't belong to me. I knelt in front of Colt, my eyes tracing the gash along his arm where Scar's knife had caught him.

"Let me see," I whispered.

He didn't protest, but his eyes—dark, haunted, alive with some storm I couldn't name—never left mine.

I tore open the first-aid kit we'd swiped from the safehouse and cleaned the wound with trembling hands. Colt hissed through his teeth as the antiseptic burned, but he didn't flinch otherwise.

"He got away," I finally said, the words tasting like ash.

Colt didn't answer right away. He leaned back, jaw tight, eyes fixed on the water-stained ceiling.

"Yeah," he said at last, voice low and jagged. "And now he knows exactly how far we're willing to go."

I sank onto the edge of the bed, my arms wrapped around myself. The motel room felt like it was closing in, every shadow a reminder of Scar's laugh, his promise echoing in my head: *This isn't over.*

"What if we can't stop him?" I asked before I could stop myself. My voice cracked on the last word.

Colt's gaze snapped to me, sharp and unyielding. "We will."

"You don't know that—"

"Yes, I do." His voice was iron, his posture shifting forward, almost predatory even in exhaustion. "Because if we don't, he'll hunt us to the ends of the earth. And I'm not letting him touch you again."

His words sent a shiver through me—part fear, part heat. The intensity in his eyes was dangerous, but it also tethered me to him like nothing else could.

I stood, pacing the narrow room, trying to bleed off the restless energy gnawing at my bones.

"Then what?" I asked. "We keep running from motel to motel, bleeding and hiding, waiting for him to make the next move?"

Colt watched me, silent, and I could see the calculation working behind his eyes. He was planning, even now, even hurt and exhausted.

"Not this time," he said finally. "He thinks he shook us. Let him believe that for a night. Tomorrow, we move first."

I stopped pacing, staring at him.

"You're talking about going on the offensive again. After everything tonight?"

He leaned forward in the chair, elbows on his knees, hands clasped like he was holding the weight of the world.

"Tonight proved one thing—we can get to him. We had him on his back, Nay. He was bleeding. He ran."

I remembered the look in Scar's eyes when Colt had the gun pressed to his forehead. He hadn't been afraid—he'd been *thrilled*. The thought sent a tremor through me.

"And if we fail next time?" I whispered.

Colt's gaze softened just slightly, his voice dropping to a low rumble. "Then we don't fail. Because I'm done running. And I'm done letting him write the rules for us."

Silence stretched between us, heavy and charged. The motel's neon sign outside the window flickered, painting his face in pulses of red and blue.

I sank onto the bed again, leaning back against the headboard, and finally let myself breathe. My whole body ached—from the fights, from the fear, from the weight of how much I wanted him in that moment.

Colt rose slowly, crossing the room with that lethal grace that still made my heart stutter. He crouched in front of me, his hands braced on the mattress.

"We'll take him apart, piece by piece," he said. "But tonight… we survive."

When his mouth met mine, it wasn't soft. It was desperate, claiming, the taste of adrenaline and blood and everything we hadn't said.

I pulled him onto the bed with me, fingers digging into his shoulders, and for a moment, the world shrank to heat and breath and the shiver of his body pressed against mine. Our clothes were damp, our skin slick with rain and sweat, but none of it mattered.

The intimacy wasn't careful this time—it was raw, tangled in exhaustion and need. Every brush of his hands over my skin reminded me we were still alive, still together, even as the world hunted us.

When it was over, we lay tangled in the dim light, the hum of the neon outside lulling me toward a fragile calm.

But sleep didn't come easy. My mind replayed Scar's laugh, his bloodied smile, and the whisper of boots on wet concrete.

We'd survived the night, but for how long?

The morning crawled in slow and gray, like the city itself wasn't sure it wanted to wake up.

I blinked against the thin sliver of light sneaking through the bent blinds and felt the weight of Colt's arm draped over my waist. His breathing was deep, even, but I could feel the heat radiating off his skin.

For a moment, I let myself stay there— wrapped in warmth that shouldn't exist after a night like that. The motel room smelled like rain-soaked clothes and cheap detergent, but there was a strange comfort in it.

Then the world crept back in. Scar's voice. Sirens. Gunshots echoing in my head.

I shifted, and Colt stirred immediately, instincts honed to a knife's edge. His hand tightened on me before his eyes even opened.

"It's morning," I said softly. "You can relax for two seconds."

His eyes opened, dark and unreadable, scanning the room before they landed on me. The edge in them softened, just barely.

"Morning's when people die," he muttered.

"Good morning to you too," I said, trying for lightness, but my voice betrayed the knot in my chest.

Colt sat up slowly, wincing as his muscles protested. The gash along his arm was swollen and angry, but he ignored it like he always did.

"We need a plan," he said, voice rough from sleep and something deeper. "We can't keep running blind."

I pushed myself up against the headboard, the thin motel blanket slipping down around my hips. The sight of him in the hazy light—rumpled, blood-streaked, unbowed—stirred something deep in me. But there wasn't time for softness.

"Scar's going to regroup," I said. "And he's going to come harder next time."

Colt nodded, already in motion. He dug through the duffel, pulling out a folded city map, a burner phone, and the black ledger he'd taken from Scar's operation weeks ago—the one we hadn't had time to crack.

I watched him spread everything across the bed, his focus razor-sharp.

"What are we looking for?" I asked.

153

"Patterns. Weak points. Somewhere we can hurt him that he won't see coming."

He flipped the ledger open, running his finger down the tight columns of numbers and street names. My eyes caught on a series of entries, each marked with a small triangle symbol in the margins.

"Wait," I said, pointing. "What's that mean?"

Colt froze for a second, then his lips curved in something that wasn't quite a smile.

"I've seen this mark before," he said. "It's his fallback stash system. Emergency cash, guns, burner IDs—enough to keep him mobile if everything else burns."

I leaned closer, my pulse picking up. "So if we hit these…"

"We cut off his escape routes," Colt finished, tapping the map with a calloused finger. "Force him into a corner he can't slither out of."

I stared at the map, tracing the points. One of them was only a few blocks from where we were hiding.

"That one," I said. "We start there. Today."

Colt glanced at me, eyebrows raised. "You sure you're ready for today?"

I held his gaze, letting the memory of last night steel me. "I was ready yesterday."

For the first time since the warehouse, he smiled—small, dangerous, and just for me.

The burner phone buzzed suddenly, slicing through the fragile calm. We both froze.

Colt grabbed it, checking the number. His jaw tightened. "Unknown."

He answered without a word, listening. His face didn't change, but I could see the shift in his eyes—the cold settling in.

He hung up after less than thirty seconds.

"Who was it?" I asked.

He hesitated. "A voice I didn't recognize. Said if we want Scar, we need to come to Pier 17 at midnight. Alone."

"Could be a trap," I said.

"It *is* a trap," Colt replied, folding the map. "But it might also be the only way to draw him out before he rebuilds."

We fell silent again, the weight of the choice pressing in.

I reached for his hand, lacing my fingers through his. "Then we make it our trap."

He met my gaze, and in that look was every promise we hadn't spoken.

Outside, a siren wailed in the distance. Inside, the city map lay between us like a contract written in blood.

By sundown, the motel room was stripped of any trace we'd been there. Colt moved like a man possessed, checking every weapon, reloading magazines, and discarding anything that might slow us down.

I packed the essentials—cash, burners, two changes of dark clothes—and every time I glanced at him, the storm in his eyes was deeper. This wasn't just preparation. This was ritual.

"You've done this before," I said, zipping the duffel.

"Too many times," Colt said without looking up. "Difference is, I've never had someone else to keep alive."

The words settled over me, a mix of heat and fear. I swallowed, tucking a knife into my boot. "Then let's make it count."

We left just after dark, the city already wearing its night mask of wet streets and humming neon. Colt drove the beat-up sedan we'd stolen from a diner parking lot, his hands steady on the wheel, while my eyes scanned every reflection in every shop window.

The streets felt alive, like they knew we were coming for blood.

Pier 17 wasn't the kind of place you stumbled onto by accident. It was tucked under the shadow of the river bridge, all rusted fencing, cracked pavement, and the sharp smell of oil and saltwater. A few fishing boats bobbed in the black water, their lights barely flickering.

We parked three blocks away, under a dead streetlight. Colt killed the engine.

"Time to disappear," he said, slipping on black gloves.

We moved through the alleys like ghosts, sticking to shadows. I followed his lead, keeping low, senses stretched tight enough to snap.

Every sound was magnified—the crunch of gravel under our boots, the distant echo of a gull, the hum of a neon sign from a liquor store across the street.

The pier came into view, lit only by a few flickering lamps and the hazy moonlight spilling over the water. It looked abandoned, but that was the trick. Nothing Scar touched was ever truly abandoned.

Colt motioned for me to wait as he crouched behind a stack of old shipping pallets, scanning the scene.

"Two on the roof," he whispered. "One by the warehouse door. Maybe more inside."

I followed his gaze and spotted the faint glint of a rifle barrel against the lamplight. My pulse jumped.

"Scar's not playing tonight," I said.

Colt's mouth tightened. "He never plays."

We spent the next hour watching.

Scar's men were disciplined, rotating in silent pairs, never straying far from the shadows. Occasionally, one would vanish into the warehouse and emerge minutes later. They were waiting for us— or someone.

I shifted against the cold metal of the pallets, careful to stay silent, and leaned into Colt's shoulder. The proximity steadied me.

"We could wait for midnight," I whispered, "but what if they expect that?"

"They *do*," Colt said. "Which is why we're not waiting."

He pointed toward a stack of old containers half-submerged in shadow along the east side of the pier.

"That's our entry. We get up to the roof, take out the sentries first, then move inside before Scar knows what's happening."

I nodded, adrenaline already singing through my blood.

We slipped through the dark like we belonged there, every step deliberate. The smell of river water and old fish clung to the air, and my boots scraped against the uneven concrete.

When we reached the containers, Colt crouched, cupping his hands.

"Up," he whispered.

I climbed onto his grip and scrambled up the container, the metal cold and slick beneath my palms. He joined me seconds later, moving with lethal ease.

From up here, the pier stretched out like a chessboard, every shadow a piece waiting to move. The sentries on the roof were silhouettes against the pale light of the river.

Colt gestured for me to hold, then slithered forward, cat-quiet. I mirrored him, breath shallow.

The first sentry never saw him coming. Colt's arm hooked around the man's throat, and the soft, wet *pop* of a silenced pistol ended it.

I grabbed the rifle before it could clatter, lowering it to the rooftop. My pulse was a roar in my ears, but we moved as one.

The second sentry turned just in time to see me.

Our eyes met for a split second—then I pulled the trigger. The silenced shot dropped him without a sound.

Colt's hand brushed my back. "Good."

From this vantage, we could see everything. The single guard at the warehouse door leaned lazily against the frame, his posture screaming boredom.

Colt's eyes locked on him. "He's next."

I nodded, my throat dry.

Then movement caught my eye.

Across the street from the pier, in the reflection of a dirty storefront window, headlights flared. Two black SUVs crept into view, their engines low, their windows tinted.

My gut twisted. "We've got company."

Colt followed my gaze, his face hardening. "Scar brought reinforcements. He's expecting a war."

The clock in my head started ticking. Every second we stayed on that roof, the net tightened.

"We move now," Colt said. "Or we don't move at all."

I swallowed my fear and nodded.

Colt's eyes locked with mine across the rooftop, the city's glow catching in his dark irises like an omen.

"This is it," he whispered.

I nodded, steadying my breathing. *No more running.*

We slid across the slick metal roof toward the hatch that led into the warehouse. Colt knelt beside it, gloved hands brushing away a thin film of grime before he eased it open. A faint creak groaned against the night air, but the wind off the river masked the sound.

The smell hit first.

Oil. Dust. Rust. And the faintest metallic tang of blood.

Jahari Hasahi Malik

Colt went first, lowering himself into the darkness like he'd done this a hundred times. I followed, boots finding the ladder rungs, the void below swallowing me whole.

Inside, the warehouse was a cathedral of shadows. Shafts of moonlight pierced the broken windows, illuminating the ribs of old steel beams and stacked shipping crates. The echo of the river outside was a heartbeat in the distance.

We crouched behind a stack of boxes, our breathing low and controlled. The single door guard we'd spotted earlier was pacing the far aisle now, humming to himself. He had no idea the roof above him was already ours.

Colt leaned close, his lips a breath from my ear.
"You take left. I'll take right. We meet at the floor level and push to the office."

I nodded, adrenaline already burning through me like fire.

We split.

My boots touched the concrete floor silently, every muscle coiled tight. The warehouse smelled of river rot and iron. My pistol felt heavier than it should, but I kept it up, scanning, moving.

The guard's shadow flickered against the wall as he turned the corner into my line of sight.

I didn't hesitate.

A soft exhale, a squeeze of the trigger, and the silenced shot hit home. He crumpled without a word, the hum of his song cut short.

Colt appeared from the other side, already moving to drag the body behind a crate. His efficiency was terrifying and oddly reassuring all at once.

We advanced deeper, using the crates as cover. From somewhere in the belly of the building, muffled voices drifted—Scar's men, laughing, arguing, alive and unaware that their night had already started to die.

Then a door slammed.

We froze.

Scar stepped out of the upstairs office like he'd been waiting for us the whole time. He was alone, no weapon in hand, but his presence filled the space like gasoline waiting for a spark.

"Thought I smelled desperation," he said, his voice carrying in the hollow room. "You two really don't know when to quit, do you?"

Colt straightened, gun aimed. "End of the line, Scar."

Scar laughed, slow and smooth.

"The end of the line? Baby girl,"—his eyes cut to me—"this is *my* city. You're just passing through."

Movement flickered behind him—two more men stepping out, rifles in hand.

Colt fired first.

The warehouse exploded into chaos.

Bullets punched through crates and ricocheted off steel. I dove behind cover, the burn of adrenaline flooding my veins. Splinters rained down as one of Scar's men shredded the box I was crouched behind.

Colt returned fire, methodical and merciless. One man fell from the catwalk above, landing with a sickening thud.

Scar had vanished into the maze of shadows, his laugh echoing like a ghost.

I moved fast, rolling to the next stack of crates, and caught a glimpse of him sprinting toward the back office.

"Colt!" I shouted, firing at the last gunman and dropping him. "He's heading for the exit!"

Colt vaulted the crate, landing beside me, his face set in grim focus.

"We finish this," he said.

We chased Scar through the warehouse, the echoes of our footsteps and gunfire bouncing off the steel walls. My lungs burned, but I didn't slow.

Scar ducked through a side door, and we followed into a narrow hallway that stank of river water and rust. He was fast—faster than a man with this much blood on his hands had any right to be—but Colt was faster.

We cornered him at the end of the hall, where the door to the pier gaped open to the cold night.

Scar finally raised his hands, his chest heaving, a wolfish grin on his face.

"Guess this is the part where you kill me," he said. "But let me ask you… then what?"

His words hung in the air, dripping with something dangerous, almost prophetic.

Colt didn't answer. He didn't have to. His finger tightened on the trigger.

Scar lunged.

The struggle was brutal and close, all fists, elbows, and the grunts of men who had run out of words. I dove into the fight, swinging the butt of my gun into Scar's ribs. He snarled, twisted, and slammed me against the doorframe hard enough to make the world flicker white.

Colt tackled him, and the three of us crashed into the wet night air, rolling onto the concrete pier.

The river lapped below, black and bottomless.

Scar managed to grab Colt's collar, dragging him toward the edge.

"You don't get to win," he spat.

Colt headbutted him, hard, and Scar reeled back, just long enough for me to bring my gun up.

One shot.

Scar stumbled.

Another.

He toppled into the river with a splash that was swallowed almost instantly by the dark.

We stood there panting, the night suddenly silent except for the rush of blood in my ears.

Colt's hand found mine, warm and shaking.

"Not over," he said.

And I knew he was right. Somewhere in that black water, Scar's shadow still lingered.

Chapter 14 Blood Oath

The night air tasted like metal and rain. My hands wouldn't stop shaking, even though the gun was finally lowered. Colt and I stood at the edge of Pier 17, the river swallowing Scar in its cold black mouth, ripples fading like he'd never been there at all.

The city around us hummed in its usual restless rhythm—distant sirens, a foghorn low and mournful—but for a moment, it felt like the world had gone silent, waiting for us to breathe again.

Colt's hand slid into mine, warm despite the bite of the river air. He didn't look triumphant. He looked tired. Haunted.

"You okay?" he asked, voice rough.

"I… don't know." My words came out shaky, like they were borrowed from someone else. "It's over, right?"

Colt's jaw tightened. He stared at the water, where the moon cast a broken reflection. "Maybe."

We didn't wait to see if the river gave Scar back.

The getaway car was three blocks away, hidden under a dead streetlight. We ran through the rain-slick alleys, hearts pounding in a rhythm that matched the slap of our boots on the concrete. Every shadow felt like it reached for us, every echo like Scar's laugh still clinging to the walls of the city.

When we finally reached the car, Colt yanked the door open for me, and we slipped inside. He started the engine, and the purr of the motor sounded too loud. Too alive.

As the tires hissed over wet asphalt, I stared at my reflection in the passenger window. My braid was fraying, blood smeared across my cheek like a warning I couldn't wipe away.

Scar was gone.

But I didn't feel free.

The motel room was a shell of comfort when we returned. We didn't turn on the lights—just kicked off our boots and fell into the shadows. I peeled off my jacket, feeling the dried rain and sweat cling to my skin.

Colt dropped his bag by the bed and leaned against the wall, silent. His chest rose and fell slowly, like he was keeping himself from unraveling.

"We did it," I said finally, breaking the heavy quiet. "Scar's gone. He can't—"

"He's not gone."

I froze. "I saw him fall."

Colt's gaze met mine, dark and unflinching. "You think a man like Scar dies easy? He's like a stain. He's in the water now, but until I see a body, I'm not calling this over."

The words chilled me more than the rain ever could.

I walked to him, touching his chest where his heart hammered beneath damp cotton.
"Then what do we do?"

His hand covered mine, calloused and steady. "We prepare for round two. And we move fast. Because if Scar lives... he's not coming alone next time."

I wanted to argue, to cling to the fragile relief of thinking it was finished. But deep down, I knew Colt was right. That victory I thought I felt on the pier—it was slipping away, bleeding out like the river had swallowed it whole.

Later, when the adrenaline finally started to drain from my veins, exhaustion hit like a tidal wave. Colt slid into the bed behind me, pulling me into his arms. His warmth and the steady thrum of his heart anchored me, but even in his embrace, sleep felt fragile.

In the thin slivers of moonlight spilling through the blinds, I thought about Scar's grin, the way he'd asked, *Then what?*

I didn't have an answer.

Somewhere deep in the city, an engine roared. Tires squealed. My eyes snapped open.

Colt was already sitting up, reaching for his gun.

"You hear that?"

A beat of silence.

Then the unmistakable echo of a car door slamming.

Colt's eyes found mine in the dark.

"He's not done with us."

Morning didn't feel like morning.

It crept in slow and gray, dripping through the blinds in pale streaks that painted the cheap motel walls. I woke to the faint hum of the heater and the scent of Colt's cologne clinging to my shirt. For a moment, in that fragile bubble of half-sleep, I almost let myself believe we were safe.

Then the memories came back. The river. Scar's grin. The splash that didn't feel like an ending.

I rolled over to find Colt already awake, sitting at the edge of the bed with his gun across his lap. He was shirtless, muscles taut, his eyes fixed on the window like he could see straight through it to the city beyond.

"You haven't slept." My voice was rough, breaking the silence like a guilty whisper.

He shook his head slowly. "Can't."

I pushed up on one elbow, letting the blanket slip down my shoulder. "You think he's still out there."

Colt glanced at me then, and the look in his eyes told me everything I didn't want to hear. "I *know* he is."

The tension between us wasn't sharp—it was quiet, heavy, like smoke after a fire. I swung my legs off the bed and sat beside him, close enough that our thighs brushed. He leaned into my warmth almost instinctively, the weight of the night before still coiled around his shoulders.

"What now?" I asked.

Colt ran a hand over his face, rough with stubble.
"Now we move. We can't sit here waiting for him to find us. We'll track his network, cut him off piece by piece until there's nothing left but him."

I swallowed hard. That kind of plan didn't feel like victory. It felt like war.
"And if he comes first?"

167

Colt's mouth curved into something that wasn't quite a smile.
"Then he won't leave."

I stood and crossed to the small motel bathroom. The mirror was streaked, the light too harsh, but I still studied the reflection staring back at me. My braid was a mess, my cheek still marked by the faint smear of blood from last night. My eyes looked older. Harder.

Colt appeared in the doorway, leaning against the frame. His gaze swept over me in that way that always made my stomach twist—like he saw the whole of me, bruises and all.

"You're thinking too loud," he said.

I exhaled. "I'm thinking about how easy it was to believe it was over. For five minutes, I thought... maybe we could breathe."

He stepped into the bathroom, closing the distance between us. His hand found my waist, grounding me.

"I'll make sure we can," he murmured. "Just not yet."

The intimacy came like gravity, pulling us into each other. His lips found mine, slow but desperate, like he needed this to remember he was alive. I melted into him, feeling the raw edges of fear and adrenaline dissolve into heat.

When he lifted me onto the counter, the cold tile under my thighs, I let my hands explore the ridges of his shoulders, the steady thrum of his heartbeat beneath calloused skin. This wasn't just passion—it was survival. A way to hold back the world, if only for a few minutes.

Afterward, we stayed tangled for a moment, foreheads touching, breaths uneven. It was quiet except for the hum of the heater and the soft patter of rain against the window.

Then Colt's phone buzzed.

He didn't answer immediately. He just stared at it like the world on the other side of that screen might be a loaded gun. Finally, he swiped to read the message.

His jaw clenched.

"It's Tino."

My stomach dropped.

"What does he want?"

Colt hesitated. "He says Scar's crew has been spotted near the river. And… there's chatter that someone matching Scar's description was seen limping into the old ferry tunnels."

I felt the blood drain from my face. "He survived."

Colt slipped the phone into his pocket, already reaching for his gear.

"I told you. Men like Scar don't drown easy."

We packed quickly. The sun hadn't even fully broken through the clouds, but the city was already awake, restless. When we stepped out of the motel, the wet streets gleamed under the weak daylight, and for a heartbeat, it felt like the whole city was holding its breath, waiting to see who would bleed first.

The city changed once you started hunting it.

Every corner, every shadow felt like it was watching back. Colt drove with the radio off, engine humming low, his eyes always moving—rearview, side mirror, the fractured reflections in the glass towers we passed. I sat next to him, my heart thudding in quiet rhythm with the wipers cutting arcs across the drizzle-streaked windshield.

We didn't talk much. Words felt heavy, like they'd fall into the silence and give us away.

We ditched the car five blocks from the river and continued on foot. The air was damp and metallic, thick with the scent of oil and rusted iron. The closer we got to the ferry tunnels, the quieter the city became.

It was the kind of quiet that didn't belong.

The tunnels had been closed for decades, ever since a fire gutted the old ferry dock and left the underbelly of the river like a skeleton. Locals whispered about the place—how gangs used it for drops, how bodies sometimes surfaced downstream after storms.

Colt checked his Glock, sliding a fresh mag in with a soft click. "Stay sharp," he murmured.

I nodded, tightening my grip on the small pistol he'd given me, feeling its weight settle into my palm like a cold promise.

The entrance to the tunnels yawned like a broken mouth at the edge of the riverbank, half-hidden behind a wall of chain-link and dead ivy. A faded *NO TRESPASSING* sign swung on one hinge, clanging softly in the wind.

Colt cut the chain in two swift motions, the links falling with a muted rattle. He pushed the gate open just wide enough for us to slip inside.

The darkness swallowed us whole.

Inside, the air was colder, and the smell of stagnant water clung to everything. Our footsteps echoed off concrete walls slick with condensation.

Colt held up a small tactical flashlight, the narrow beam cutting through the shadows. Graffiti sprawled across the walls in jagged letters, old tags mixed with fresh ones. Some had been crossed out with red spray paint, warnings layered over warnings.

We found a dry ledge and crouched, eyes scanning the black water below and the passages that snaked deeper into the earth.

"Patience," Colt whispered, his voice almost lost in the dripping of water somewhere in the dark.

Surveillance in the tunnels was different from watching rooftops or alleyways. Out here, the shadows could breathe. Every sound traveled and warped. A splash from far down the corridor could sound like it was right behind us.

For hours, we watched.

At one point, faint voices echoed from deeper in the tunnels. I strained to listen, catching fragments—a laugh, a cough, a sharp bark of orders. Scar's men.

I tensed, but Colt rested a steadying hand on my knee.

"Not yet," he whispered.

In the stillness, the intimacy crept in. His hand lingered, a silent anchor in the void. I leaned into his shoulder, drawing comfort from the solid heat of him. Even here, surrounded by damp concrete and the ghost of danger, he was gravity.

It was a dangerous kind of closeness—one that could get us killed if we forgot the world outside our bubble. But in that moment, with the city's underbelly breathing around us, I needed it.

Movement.

A single flashlight flickered at the far end of the tunnel, cutting across the water like a jagged knife. Two figures emerged from the shadows, rifles slung across their chests. They moved with the kind of restless alertness that came from expecting trouble.

Scar's men.

We crouched lower, silent as stone, watching them disappear into a side corridor.

Colt exhaled slowly, lips near my ear. "He's here."

Back in the daylight, we'd parked a second vehicle nearby, stashed with gear and enough ammo for a small war. Colt's plan was clear now—track Scar to his lair, map out his operation, and wait for the perfect moment to end this before he could rebuild.

But the longer we watched, the clearer it became: Scar was already rebuilding.

Men came and went. Supplies were hauled in. We even caught a glimpse of a black SUV idling near the river entrance, a silent sentinel waiting for orders.

I gritted my teeth. "He's setting up for something big."

Colt's jaw flexed. "Then we take it from him before it starts."

Hours later, we finally retreated, slipping back into the night like ghosts. The city lights beyond the river looked colder than ever, fractured and distant.

Back in the car, Colt laid a rough map across the dashboard, marking the tunnel entrances and the spots we'd seen men move. His handwriting was quick and sharp, like he was etching war plans into the page.

"Tomorrow," he said, glancing at me. "We hit them tomorrow night. Before they realize we're already inside their skin."

I nodded, but inside, I could feel the storm building. Tomorrow wasn't a promise—it was a warning.

Night returned like a promise we couldn't ignore.

The city glimmered under rain-polished streets, lights fractured in puddles, and the hum of traffic muffled by the wind sweeping off the river. Colt parked two blocks away from the old ferry tunnels, killing the engine and letting the quiet settle in.

We sat in the dark for a moment, neither of us speaking, listening to the pulse of our own breathing.

"You ready?" Colt's voice was low, steady, like the steel in his gun.

I nodded, my fingers tightening around the grip of my pistol.

"Let's end this."

We moved like shadows through the alleys, damp brick under our fingertips, the smell of rain and river water thick in the air. The chain-link gate we'd cut earlier still sagged in place, creaking softly as we slipped inside.

The tunnels swallowed us again.

But this time, the air was alive with the murmur of voices and the faint clang of metal echoing off concrete. Flashlights bobbed in the distance, slicing the dark in uneven arcs.

Colt motioned for me to follow as he crouched low, hugging the wall. We weaved through the shadows, moving from one pool of darkness to the next, our boots silent on the damp floor.

The first man didn't even have time to cry out.

Colt came up behind him, hand over his mouth, and drove him into the wall with a quiet thud. The second man turned too late—I took the shot, the sound sharp but swallowed quickly by the tunnels. He collapsed into the shallow water, sending ripples out like a warning.

Colt glanced back at me, eyes gleaming in the dim light.

"Nice," he mouthed.

We pressed deeper.

Scar's crew had turned the tunnels into something between a staging ground and a fortress. Crates lined the ledges, some stenciled with black letters I couldn't make out in the dark. The smell of gasoline hung heavy, mingling with the rot of the river.

We heard laughter before we saw him.

Scar's voice slithered through the dark like a taunt. "Thought you could wash me away, Colt?"

I froze, pulse hammering.

Colt's grip tightened around my hand briefly before he let go and stepped forward, his voice carrying low and cold.

"You should've stayed down."

Scar stepped into the cone of light cast by a dangling work lamp. His clothes were damp and stained, his face a map of bruises, but his grin was untouched. Behind him, three men flanked the crates, rifles in hand.

"Well, ain't this sweet," Scar drawled. "The lovebirds come to finish the job themselves. Romantic."

His gaze flicked to me, slow and deliberate, making my stomach twist.

"Tell me, girl—he worth all this running?"

I raised my gun. "Ask yourself if you are."

Scar laughed, a low, rasping sound that echoed off the walls.

"Feisty. I like that. Shame you crawled into his bed instead of mine."

The tension snapped like a live wire.

Colt fired first, a deafening crack that lit up the darkness. The tunnels exploded into chaos— gunfire ricocheting, shouts echoing in the confined space, the stink of cordite mixing with the river's stench. I dropped behind a crate, returning fire as Scar's men scattered for cover.

175

Water splashed as someone charged. I swung my pistol and fired, the man crumpling into the black water.

Colt moved like a predator, low and precise, every shot a promise. But Scar was fast, darting behind crates, his laughter cutting through the noise like a knife.

"You think you can kill me down here?" he shouted. "This is *my* river, Colt!"

I felt movement behind me—another man lunging from the shadows. Before I could react, Colt was there, his fist connecting with a wet, meaty crack. The man hit the floor, and Colt yanked me close, shielding me as another burst of gunfire rained against the crates.

We were breathing hard, soaked from spray and sweat, hearts syncing to the chaos around us. For a split second, his eyes met mine—a flash of heat, fear, and something like home—even here, in hell.

Then Scar's voice came again, closer now. "I'm gonna carve you outta each other," he growled.

Colt's jaw set. He handed me a spare clip. "Stay with me."

We advanced through the maze of crates and echoing corridors, guns raised, every nerve on fire.

Finally, we cornered him near a collapsed section of the tunnel where water cascaded from a broken pipe. Scar stood framed in the spray, gun in one hand, knife in the other, his grin wide and wild.

"This the part where we finish it?" he asked.

Colt's voice was ice.

"Yeah. This is it."

Love is a Loaded Clip

The three of us faced off in the dripping dark,
the river's heartbeat all around, and I knew—
whatever happened next would decide everything.

Chapter 15 No Safe Place in the Tunnels

The tunnel felt alive, breathing in sync with the storm of violence that raged inside it. Water dripped from the broken pipe above, tapping out a rhythm that seemed to mock the standoff.

My pulse beat faster than the drops, hammering in my ears, drowning out everything but Scar's grin in the half-light.

He was circling now, slow and deliberate, a predator tasting the air. His boots sloshed through the shallow water, leaving ripples that spread toward us like warnings.

Colt kept his gun trained on him, but even I could see his knuckles were pale against the grip. This wasn't the kind of fight you could win with a clean shot. This was the kind that left scars, no matter how it ended.

Scar licked his teeth and gestured with the knife, its blade catching the light.

"Pretty little mouse," he said, eyes sliding to me. "You've been running through my tunnels like you own 'em. Hiding behind your man like that gun's gonna save you."

I felt the words hit, felt the anger and fear coil in my gut. I raised my pistol higher, two hands steady despite the tremor in my chest. "I'm not hiding," I said.

Scar laughed, the sound bouncing off the wet concrete walls like something feral.
"That right? Then step up, sweetheart. Show me you ain't just a shadow he drags along."

Before I could answer, he lunged.

The world snapped into chaos. Colt fired, the muzzle flash lighting the tunnel for a heartbeat of clarity. The bullet chipped the wall near Scar's head, spraying wet concrete dust into the air. Scar was already moving, a blur of damp leather and muscle, and slammed into Colt with a force that rattled my bones just from watching.

I stumbled back, pistol up, but they were a tangle of motion—Colt grunting, Scar swinging that knife in brutal arcs. The tunnel amplified everything: the scrape of boots, the splash of water, the echo of every ragged breath.

"Move, Nay!" Colt shouted, straining under Scar's weight.

I moved. Instinct took over. I circled to the side, heart in my throat, searching for an opening. Scar had Colt pinned against a slick wall, his knife flashing toward his ribs. Colt blocked with his forearm, teeth clenched in pain, and managed to slam his elbow into Scar's jaw. The man barely flinched.

I had a clean shot—except I didn't. Colt was in the way, the angles bad. One wrong move, and I'd be the one to put him down.

Think.

Scar swung again, and Colt twisted, barely avoiding the blade. Their bodies splashed into the shallow water, sending icy droplets across my face. I caught Scar's shadow flicker against the wall and fired. The shot grazed his shoulder, spinning him just enough for Colt to shove him off.

Scar staggered, blood darkening his sleeve. He looked at me and grinned wider, like the pain fed him.

"That's more like it," he hissed.
Then he came for me.

I froze for a fraction too long, and suddenly Scar was in my space, all teeth and steel. I ducked under the first slash, my shoulder grazing the wet wall. He grabbed my arm with a hand like iron, yanking me forward into the dark water up to my knees. My gun slipped in my grip, the cold stealing my breath.

Colt roared, slamming into Scar's back. They went down together, a thrashing mess of fists, elbows, and splashing water. I scrambled up, shaking, lungs tight with panic and adrenaline.

I saw the knife flash again. Scar was on top, pressing it down toward Colt's throat.

"No!"

I threw myself forward, grabbing Scar's arm with both hands and yanking hard. He twisted toward me, rage in his eyes, and Colt seized the opening—his fist cracking against Scar's jaw with a sound that echoed like a gunshot.

Scar reeled, and for the first time, I saw real anger break through his smugness. He spat blood into the water, breathing hard.

"Alright," he growled, voice like gravel. "No more playin'."

He lunged for me again, faster than I expected. His hand clamped around my throat, cold and merciless, and he shoved me back against the wall. My pistol clattered to the floor, sliding into the water. The knife pressed against my cheek, its edge biting just enough to sting.

"You feel that?" he whispered, low enough only I could hear. "One slip, and you're gone. And he—" he jerked his head toward Colt— "he's gonna watch."

Fear flared hot in my chest, but something else rose with it—a spark of defiance. He wanted me helpless, terrified. He wanted me small.

I refused to give him that.

"Colt!" I gasped, just as Scar shifted to enjoy his moment.

That single second of gloating was his mistake. Colt barreled into him with the force of a freight train, ripping me free from Scar's grip.

The three of us went down hard, water spraying in icy sheets. My fingers closed around something—my gun, slick but solid—and I spun onto my knees.

Scar came up swinging, his knife arcing through the dark. I didn't think. I aimed and fired.

The shot tore through the tunnel, deafening in the confined space. Scar jerked, stumbled, and fell into the water with a splash that sent ripples racing down the corridor.

He wasn't dead. Not yet. But he was bleeding, scrambling toward the shadows, leaving a trail we could follow straight into hell.

Colt pulled me up, his hands rough but steady, his eyes scanning my face like he couldn't believe I was still standing.

"You alright?"

I nodded, though my hands shook, my heart a wild drumbeat. "I'm not letting him take me. Not now. Not ever."

Colt's mouth twitched—half pride, half fear—as he glanced down the tunnel where Scar had fled.

"Then we finish this."

And as we plunged deeper into the wet, echoing dark, I realized this fight wasn't just survival anymore. It was transformation. If I came out of this alive, I'd never be the same girl who walked into these tunnels.

We staggered into the abandoned locker room near the tunnel's service exit, soaked to the bone, dripping water and blood onto cracked tile floors. The flickering light from a single overhead bulb painted us in fractured shadows, our breaths harsh and ragged in the cold air.

Colt slammed the rusted door shut and slid the bolt with a metallic clang. The echo swallowed us in silence except for the water running down our clothes and the frantic rhythm of my pulse.

For a moment, neither of us moved. We were animals coming down from a hunt, both alive only because the other had refused to die.

Then Colt crossed the room in two strides and grabbed me, his mouth crushing against mine.

It wasn't soft.

It was desperate.

The taste of blood and river water mixed with heat, and I clung to him like he was the only thing tethering me to the world. My back hit the damp tile wall, the cold shock racing up my spine even as his hands set my skin on fire.

Every nerve in my body woke up, raw and hungry.

His mouth trailed along my jaw, rough stubble scraping in a way that made me shiver. I could feel the restrained violence in him, the heat under the ice he always wore, and it matched the chaos in my chest perfectly.

"God, Nay…" he whispered against my neck, voice jagged, "I almost lost you back there."

"You didn't," I breathed, gripping his shirt, yanking him closer. "I'm right here. I'm *yours*."

The words lit something behind his eyes, something feral. His hands slid under my soaked shirt, fingers tracing the curve of my spine, pressing against my trembling skin. My breath hitched, my body arching into him, craving him the same way I craved survival.

When his lips found mine again, the kiss deepened—less desperate now, but raw, a slow claiming. He tasted like danger, like home, like the only thing in this cold, merciless city that was mine to keep.

I let my hands explore him in return, the hard planes of his chest under wet fabric, the steady thrum of his heartbeat beneath my palm. He smelled like rain, gunpowder, and the faint, metallic tang of blood.

We were a mess—filthy, hunted, exhausted— but right here, pressed against the wall with his breath in my ear, I'd never felt more alive.

He pulled back just enough to look at me, his thumb brushing the corner of my mouth, a smear of dirt following the motion.

"I can't keep you safe if you keep putting yourself in the line of fire," he said, his voice a low growl, thick with both fear and desire.

I shook my head, my hand sliding to the back of his neck, holding him close.

"I don't want safe, Colt. I want *us*—whatever it costs."

The answer came in the way he lifted me, effortlessly, my legs wrapping around his waist as he carried me to the old wooden bench against the wall. It creaked under our weight, the sound almost lost under the pounding in my chest.

He kissed me again, slower now, letting the heat smolder instead of burn outright, his hands exploring my curves with the kind of focus he saved for a loaded weapon. Every touch said *you're mine* and *don't you dare leave me* all at once.

The outside world felt far away for those stolen minutes. No Scar. No tunnels. No death waiting around the corner.

Just Colt's hands on my skin, the steady rhythm of his body against mine, and the rare, quiet way he whispered my name like it was a prayer he hadn't known he needed to say.

"Nay…" His voice broke, rough with something deeper than lust. "I swear, after this… I'll get us out. Somewhere we can breathe."

I ran my fingers through his damp hair, forcing his gaze to meet mine.
"Then make me believe it."

He kissed me again, and the world fell away.

We lingered there longer than we should have, lost in the heat and the heartbeat of each other, until reality crept back in with a distant metallic clang from the tunnels below. The sound sliced through the haze like a warning bell.

Colt froze, every muscle tight, listening.

"They're regrouping," he said, setting me down gently but firmly. His hands stayed on my hips for one more heartbeat, unwilling to let go.

"I know." I forced my voice steady, swallowing the lump in my throat. "Then we finish this."

He nodded, his thumb brushing my lower lip one last time.

"Together."

And just like that, the heat of our stolen moment hardened into resolve. We grabbed our guns, adjusted our wet clothes, and stepped back into the nightmarish tunnel labyrinth—hearts still racing for reasons beyond fear.

The echoes came first.

A distant clang of metal, sharp and hollow, bouncing through the tunnels like a warning we were already too late to heed.

Colt raised a hand, signaling me to stop, his eyes scanning the dark corridor ahead. The sound of dripping water had shifted—no longer random. Footsteps, careful and deliberate, matched the rhythm now.

I swallowed hard, gripping my pistol tighter, feeling the ghosts of Colt's hands still on my skin. Our raw, stolen moment clung to me like heat under my clothes, but the icy fingers of fear were crawling back in fast.

"Left or right?" I whispered.

Colt glanced at the map etched in his memory, then pointed left. "Quieter. But it's a dead end if we're wrong."

We moved, footsteps silent in the ankle-deep water, the air thick with mildew and electricity. Every shadow seemed alive, every flicker of light from the broken bulbs above like a taunt. I could almost *feel* Scar's men behind us—hunters in the dark, closing in.

A soft scrape made me freeze. Metal on concrete.

Colt heard it too. His hand brushed mine— steady, grounding—and then he lifted his gun toward the narrow bend ahead.

The tunnel suddenly bloomed with light.

A flashlight beam cut through the dark like a blade, catching the glint of wet walls and casting monstrous shadows. I ducked behind a concrete support as Colt slid beside me.

"Two," he mouthed.

I risked a glance. He was right. Two of Scar's men, dressed in dark hoodies and soaked jeans, moved carefully through the water, guns raised.

They were close enough for me to see the tension in their jaws, the subtle tremor of men who'd been ordered into hell and knew it.

A memory of Scar's grip on my throat surfaced, cold and visceral, and rage pushed through the fear. I wasn't prey anymore. Not after everything.

Colt leaned close, his breath hot against my ear.

"On my mark."

I nodded.

He counted silently—one… two…

The third beat was gunfire.

Colt's first shot was a whisper of light in the darkness, hitting the lead man clean in the chest. The second man panicked, spinning with his flashlight, and I took the opening—my shot clipped his leg, dropping him into the water with a splash that echoed down the corridor.

We didn't wait to finish him. Colt grabbed my wrist, yanking me through the shadows, deeper into the labyrinth. Behind us, the wounded man cursed and called out, his voice echoing until it seemed like it came from everywhere at once.

We ran until the tunnels forked again, both paths swallowed in black. I bent double, hands on my knees, the cold air cutting into my lungs. Colt pressed against the wall, listening, his face set in stone.

"They're spreading out," he said finally.

"Like rats," I whispered.

The water at my feet rippled. My stomach dropped. "Colt…"

He followed my gaze just in time to see a beam of light snake along the tunnel floor—a reflection of someone's flashlight approaching from behind.

"Go!" he hissed.

We sprinted. My boots splashed through the water, every step an echoing alarm. The tunnels twisted like a maze, the darkness pressing close, and for a moment it felt like the walls were breathing with us—alive, waiting for someone to fail.

Another light flared ahead.

Trapped.

We skidded to a halt in a narrow junction, hemmed in by rusted pipes and the slick hum of dripping water. My chest heaved, my skin hot despite the cold, and the memory of Colt's hands on me earlier only made the terror sharper. This wasn't just life or death anymore—it was *everything we could have had, ripped away* if we failed here.

"Listen to me," Colt whispered, pulling me into the shadow of a side alcove. His hand pressed over mine on the gun, steadying the tremor in my fingers. "We don't panic. We control the dark."

I nodded, letting his voice anchor me, even as footsteps grew louder on both sides.

Then came the whistle.

Low, eerie, and unmistakable. Scar's call.

It crawled under my skin, a sound that belonged to predators, and the tunnel seemed to answer with silence before the chaos hit.

The first man rounded the corner, flashlight cutting across the alcove. Colt's arm tightened around me like a shield as he fired. The shot lit up the darkness for a heartbeat, showing another figure behind the first—then the beam went spinning into the water.

Shouts erupted. Gunfire barked back, the noise deafening in the enclosed space. Water sprayed up around us as bullets struck the surface, sending ripples of icy shock across my boots.

"Move!" Colt shoved me forward as we dashed into another side passage, the world a blur of shadow and light. I felt the walls scrape my shoulders, smelled the sour mix of rust and river filth, and heard Scar's whistle echo again—closer this time.

"They're herding us," I realized aloud.

"I know," Colt said, grim. His eyes were sharp even in the dark, every sense on high alert.

A sudden crash behind us made my heart lurch. Metal clattered against stone, and then— silence.

Too quiet.

The air was thick with the scent of gunpowder and something older, something foul. My grip on my pistol tightened as I realized this wasn't just a fight anymore. It was a hunt, and Scar's men knew the tunnels better than we did.

And Scar was coming.

A shadow flickered at the edge of my vision. I spun, gun raised, heart hammering—but nothing. Just wet walls and the whisper of water.

"Stay close," Colt murmured. He wasn't asking.

Every nerve in my body was on fire, hyperaware. The memory of Colt's touch, his voice in my ear, his weight against mine—it was all still there, making my pulse trip over itself. But now it sharpened into something else: fear, anger, and the primal need to survive.

From the darkness ahead, a voice slid through the air like smoke.

"You can't run forever, sweet thing."

Scar.

The words froze my blood.

And for the first time since we entered the tunnels, I wondered if this was where one of us wouldn't walk out.

Scar's voice slithered through the tunnels, bouncing off the damp stone like the city itself was mocking me.

"You can't run forever, sweet thing."

Colt's hand brushed my arm, grounding me.

His jaw was a granite wall, his eyes sharp even in the flickering dark. He wasn't just fighting for survival now—he was hunting. For me. For *us*.

The tunnel ahead narrowed to a choke point where two old service doors sat crooked on their hinges. I felt the shift in Colt's stance before he said a word.

"He's driving us into his box," Colt muttered.

"Then let's break the damn box," I whispered back, heat rising in my chest.

We slid into the tight corridor. My heart was a war drum in my ears. Then—silence.

A shadow peeled itself from the dark like it had been waiting.

Scar.

His eyes gleamed like wet asphalt under a streetlight, his knife glinting as if it had been forged from the city's hate. The ragged scar across his jaw caught the pale tunnel light, and the smirk on his face was pure venom.

"Well, look who crawled out of the gutter," he said, voice low and almost amused. "I was starting to think you two were more trouble than you're worth. But now…" His gaze slid over me, deliberate, invasive. "…I think I'll take my time."

Colt didn't flinch, but I felt the fire in him. He stepped slightly in front of me, gun raised, a living wall of fury.

"Touch her, and it's the last thing you do."

Scar chuckled, slow and lazy, as if he'd already won. "You think you're the first man to make that promise in this city?" He tilted his head, knife spinning in his hand. "They all end up the same—face down, and she's screaming for me anyway."

Rage sliced through the fear like a blade. I stepped out from Colt's shadow, leveling my pistol.

"Try me, Scar."

The smirk faded just a fraction. Then, with a snap of his fingers, the tunnels came alive.

Footsteps thundered in the distance. Lights flickered on—flashlights, swinging wildly—casting us all in a nightmare strobe. Colt fired first, his bullet sparking off Scar's knife as he twisted away with inhuman speed.

Chaos detonated.

Scar lunged, knife flashing. Colt blocked him with his forearm, the blade skimming flesh, and the sound of metal against bone made my stomach flip. I fired at the shadow behind him—one of Scar's men—dropping him into the water with a splash that echoed like thunder.

The tunnel became a cage of screams, gunshots, and steel.

Scar was fast—too fast. He ducked under Colt's swing, slashed upward, and Colt hissed as the knife nicked his ribs. Blood sprayed warm against my cheek.

"Colt!"

"I'm good," he gritted out, shoving Scar back with a brutal shoulder check that cracked against stone.

Another man came at me from the side. I didn't think—I just spun, letting my fear and anger guide me. My shot caught him in the chest. He fell without a sound.

For a second, the world tunneled into just three people: Colt, Scar, and me. Every drip of water, every pulse in my neck, every whisper of movement felt magnified.

Scar came at me next.

He didn't aim for Colt—he wanted *me*.

His hand fisted in my shirt, yanking me close, the cold blade grazing my skin as his voice slid against my ear.

"Should've stayed in your lane, princess."

I slammed my knee into his ribs, the force reverberating through my whole body. He grunted, loosening his grip, and Colt was there—slamming Scar into the wall with a fury that shook the pipes loose from their rusted brackets.

They crashed into the water, grappling like animals, Colt's gun lost to the current. The sound of fists, water, and raw rage filled the narrow space. I scrambled to grab the fallen weapon, my fingers numb and slick.

Scar got his hands on Colt's throat, pressing him against the wall, water splashing around them.

"No one walks away from me," Scar snarled, spit flying.

"Then die mad about it," Colt rasped, driving his knee upward into Scar's gut.

Scar folded for a split second—just long enough.

I fired.

The bullet tore through Scar's shoulder, spinning him into the wall with a howl that sounded more beast than man. Blood splashed into the water, warm against my legs.

Colt surged forward, ripping the knife from Scar's hand and pressing it to his throat.

"You ever touch her again," Colt said, his voice a steel whisper, "and hell will look like a mercy."

Scar froze. His chest heaved, his grin twisted and broken now—but there was no fear in his eyes. Only something worse.

"This isn't over," he hissed.

Colt hesitated. I could see it in his shoulders—the war between ending this now or letting him crawl back to whatever hole he came from. But the echo of approaching footsteps made the choice for him.

"Move!" I shouted, grabbing Colt's hand.

We ran, leaving Scar bleeding in the dark, his laughter following us like a curse.

By the time we emerged into the night, the city lights reflected off the black river like broken glass. My hands shook, my heart a riot of adrenaline and leftover desire. Colt's arm wrapped around me,

Jahari Hasahi Malik

and for a fleeting moment, we were alive and
together—but hunted still.
>   We hadn't won. Not yet.
>   But for the first time, I believed we could.

Chapter 16 Retaliation is a Must

The night swallowed us whole.

Colt's hand was a vise around mine as we stumbled through the alley, soaked to the bone, our breaths ragged clouds in the cold air. The wet slap of our boots on pavement was the only proof we were still alive, still moving, still outrunning the shadows that wanted us buried.

Behind us, the city pulsed with distant sirens and the low hum of the river. I swore I could still hear Scar's laughter threading through the night, slithering between the buildings like smoke. It was the sound of unfinished business.

We ducked into an abandoned laundromat three blocks from the ferry tunnels, the glass door hanging crooked on one hinge. Colt kicked it open with his shoulder, wincing as blood seeped through his shirt at his ribs. I followed, heart pounding, and locked the door behind us even though the rusted bolt was more symbolic than protective.

The air inside was thick with the ghost of detergent and mold. Rows of dead machines lined the walls, graffiti curling across the cracked tile like scars. A single fluorescent light flickered overhead, painting the space in fits of pale blue.

Colt slumped against a washer, breathing hard. His shirt clung to him, wet with river water and blood, and his jaw tightened when he touched the slice along his ribs.

"Let me see," I said, moving to kneel beside him.

He shook his head. "It's nothing."

"Colt." My voice left no room for argument.

He sighed and lifted his shirt. The gash was shallow but long, angry and red against the planes of his stomach. My fingers trembled as I pressed a rag I tore from an old shirt against it, the intimacy of the act nearly as raw as the violence we'd just crawled out of.

His eyes found mine, darker than I'd ever seen. "You saved my life back there."

I swallowed hard. "You saved mine first."

Silence settled between us, heavy with everything we couldn't say yet.

I'd never felt more alive or more exposed. The night outside was a predator, Scar was bleeding but far from broken, and yet… here, in this moment, with Colt watching me like I was the only reason he hadn't given up… I felt invincible.

I traced the edge of the wound gently. "You're gonna need stitches."

"You offering to play nurse?" he asked, his mouth curving into a hint of that cocky grin that always got me into trouble.

"If I have to," I said, forcing a smirk even as my stomach twisted from the close call.

His hand slid over mine, pressing it against his ribs, holding me there. The heat of his skin and the thrum of his pulse grounded me in a way words couldn't.

"I meant what I said, Nay," he murmured. "He touches you again, he dies. I don't care if the whole city burns for it."

I felt a shiver run through me—not fear, but something darker and hotter. I leaned into him, our foreheads brushing. "Then we burn it together."

The kiss was inevitable. Fierce, bruising, and desperate. A collision of everything we'd survived, everything we were fighting for, and everything we hadn't had the courage to say out loud.

His hands tangled in my wet hair, my fingers sliding over his shoulders, feeling the tension and heat in every inch of him. The taste of him—blood, rain, and stubborn resolve—was intoxicating. For a heartbeat, the world outside ceased to exist.

But the world has a way of reminding you it's still there.

The distant rumble of engines cut through the night.

Colt froze, his head snapping toward the broken window. "They're moving."

"Scar?" I asked, pulling back, adrenaline surging all over again.

"Has to be. He's not gonna lick his wounds and wait." Colt pushed himself up, grimacing but already scanning the street. "He's coming for us before we can breathe."

I grabbed my bag and checked my pistol, the memory of the tunnels burning behind my eyes.

"Then we move first."

Colt paused, studying me. There was a shift in his eyes, a recognition of something that had changed between us. I wasn't just along for the ride anymore.

"You're sure?"

"Yes," I said, my voice steady. "We finish this before he finishes us."

Outside, the engines grew louder. Headlights cut briefly across the alley, shadows stretching like claws along the walls. Scar's men weren't just hunting. They were tightening the net.

Colt nodded once. "Then we set the trap."

"How?"

He looked at me with a spark I hadn't seen in days—a dangerous, thrilling glint that promised survival through grit and audacity.

"We make him believe he's already won."

A shiver ran through me, part fear, part anticipation. The night felt like it was holding its breath, the city's heartbeat syncing with mine as I realized we were stepping into a new war.

Scar wasn't done.

Neither were we.

Blood smells different in the tunnels.

It's thicker. Metallic and wet, like the city's rusted bones are bleeding with you.

Scar leaned against the slick wall, clutching his shoulder where the bullet had kissed him. Pain pulsed through him like a second heartbeat, but he didn't let it reach his face. Pain was fuel. Pain was proof he was still alive—and that he owed someone a death for it.

The laughter that had followed Colt and Nay into the night had been real. Not joy—never that—but a promise. A dark hymn echoing in the tunnels, letting them know he wasn't beaten, not yet.

Scar straightened slowly, the pain flaring sharp and hot as he rolled his shoulder. His fingers came away slick with blood, and he studied it for a moment in the trembling light. He hated leaving any piece of himself behind, but this wasn't over. This wasn't close to over.

"Boss?" a voice rasped from the shadows.

Two of his men emerged from the dripping black, eyes wide and jittery. One was limping, the other bleeding from a graze on his temple. They looked like survivors of a war that hadn't gone their way, but Scar only saw tools—still useful, still breathing.

"Tell me you didn't lose *everyone*," he said, voice low, flat, and lethal.

The limping man shook his head fast. "Three gone. Two more outside. They're spread thin, trying to track where they ran."

Scar's jaw worked slowly as he processed it. Colt and that girl had carved through his crew like the city belonged to them.

No. He wouldn't allow it.

"They think running means surviving," Scar said, his voice curling into a hiss. "But running just tells me where to hunt."

He pushed off the wall, the tunnels stretching around him like veins in a corpse, carrying his anger forward. He thought of Colt—the grit in his jaw, the stupid, loyal way he'd thrown himself between Scar and the girl.

And the girl herself... Nay.

There was a different heat when Scar thought of her. Not just lust or rage—possession. She had *looked him in the eye* and fired, had put him on his back, and that wound burned hotter than the bullet ever could.

He wanted her screams. He wanted her silence. He wanted her under his boot or in his bed—he hadn't decided which—but he wanted her broken first.

They emerged into the night, the city air thick with damp smoke and river chill. Scar blinked against the streetlights, his wounded shoulder dragging him into a half-hunch, but he didn't stop moving.

A black SUV idled at the corner, his last loyal men perched like wolves in the dark. Scar climbed in, wincing only once as the leather stuck to the blood on his shirt.

"Where?" the driver asked.

Scar's smile was thin and cruel. "Everywhere."

As they rolled through the streets, he watched the city with a predator's patience. He knew its arteries, its safehouses, its alleys where no one asked questions and no cameras ever worked.

He knew where they would try to hide. He could smell their desperation.

He pressed his palm against his shoulder again, the heat of his own blood reminding him how close they had come to taking him out. His fingers twitched with the urge to snap Colt's neck, to drag Nay back by her hair and erase that defiance from her eyes.

"Call the rest," he ordered. "I want eyes on every exit out of my city. Sewers, alleys, rooftops—I don't care. If a rat can crawl through it, I want a man there with a gun."

The driver nodded, already tapping his phone.

"And put out the word," Scar added, leaning forward, his voice razor-sharp. "Anyone who shelters them, feeds them, breathes the same air as them— dies. I'll burn every block they touch until the streets *beg* for their blood."

One of his men hesitated. "Boss… cops'll notice if we—"

Scar's gaze sliced to him, cold and unblinking.

"Then let them notice. Let them *watch*. I'll make an example so loud the city never forgets."

He leaned back, exhaling through the pain, and the SUV turned toward the docks. He could already feel the power shifting back toward him, the city bending under his will. Colt and Nay might have survived the tunnels, but survival was just the first step in his game.

Scar's game always ended the same way.

With blood.

The first thing we noticed was the silence.

Not peace—never that. This kind of silence felt *off*, like the city was holding its breath, waiting to exhale something foul. Even the usual nighttime orchestra—the hiss of steam vents, the hum of distant engines, the buzz of neon signs—had gone quiet.

Colt noticed it first. He paused at the back door of the pawnshop we'd ducked into for shelter, his hand hovering over the knob.

"Don't like this," he muttered.

I was crouched by the boarded-up window, gun resting in my lap, trying to ignore how hard my heart was pounding. "What? The fact that it's too quiet or the fact we don't have a backup plan after this?"

He didn't answer right away. That's how I knew it was serious.

Colt didn't do nervous. He did *restless*. He paced when he was stressed, tapped his thumb against his thigh when he was thinking. But this time, he was still. Listening. Tense as a blade right before it's drawn.

"Something's coming," he said finally.

I stood, the air around us dense, the shadows stretching too long. A flicker of movement caught my eye through the broken slats—a figure, just beyond the edge of the alley. Then another. Then three more.

Colt cursed under his breath and reached for the duffel. "We're not staying here."

"Out the back?" I asked.

He nodded, tossing me a fresh clip. I caught it, loaded it into my weapon with a cold click, and shoved my braid under my hoodie.

"Go first," he said. "I'll cover—"

Glass exploded inward.

I screamed, diving to the floor as shards rained around us. Colt grabbed my arm and yanked me behind the counter just as bullets tore through the shelves. The cash register burst open in a spray of coins, the air filled with the shriek of ricochets.

"Scar's found us," I whispered.

"No," Colt growled. "He *never* lost us."

It was chaos. The back door slammed open, and Colt fired three times without hesitation. A body dropped with a wet thud just outside the threshold. I could smell the blood already, thick and coppery and hot.

We didn't have time to think.

We ran.

I kicked through the busted doorframe, heart punching my ribs, Colt right behind me. The alley was narrow, steam curling up from vents in thick waves, casting everything in a hazy blur. We ducked and wove, boots slapping puddles, our shadows breaking and reforming in the flickering orange light.

More footsteps behind us. Too many.

They weren't just chasing us—they were *herding* us.

"We're being funneled," I gasped. "Toward the main street."

"I know," Colt said. "We need height. Now."

We pivoted right and darted into a side lot, half-swallowed by debris and weeds. A rusted fire escape climbed the back of a crumbling tenement. Colt vaulted the dumpster and caught the ladder, yanking it down with a screech.

I was up first, the metal cold and slick under my fingers. By the time we hit the third floor, I heard them enter the lot below. Shouts. Muffled orders. Boots crunching glass.

Colt stopped me on the next landing and pulled me into the shadow of the stairwell. We pressed flat against the wall, his chest rising and falling against mine, both of us trembling.

"They know we're here," I whispered.

"They're not the only ones," he said—and pointed.

Across the alley, a single red laser cut the mist, landing right on Colt's shoulder.

Sniper.

We dove.

The shot cracked the air, tearing concrete where Colt's head had been a second ago. He dragged me behind a rusted HVAC unit, breath hot against my ear.

"They brought a goddamn sniper," I said, stunned.

"This isn't a warning," Colt muttered. "Scar wants a body. Tonight."

We locked eyes, and I saw it—real fear, not for himself, but for *me*. It was there in the way he scanned every ledge, every rooftop, every shadow like he could outthink a bullet.

Another shot rang out—closer this time.

"They're moving in," I said. "We can't stay up here."

"Then we drop down and disappear."

Colt took my hand, and we moved, fast and low, ducking beams of light and sliding across slick metal. The city blurred around us—just the sound of our breathing, the sting of adrenaline, the echo of every step like a war drum in my chest.

Scar wasn't playing anymore.

He was closing the net.

And this time, he wanted blood on both ends.

We barely made it out of the building alive.

Colt kicked in a maintenance door three floors down, and we dropped into a pitch-black boiler room. It smelled like rust and old oil, the air thick with heat and silence. We didn't speak. Just breathed.

Just *listened*. Boots scraped above us, and then drifted off into the night.

For now, we were ghosts.

Colt checked his weapon, then mine. His hands were trembling—just slightly—but the look in his eyes was steady.

Then his phone buzzed.

Not a text.

A call.

Blocked number. No ringtone. Just a soft vibration, like a warning growl from something too smart to lunge first.

He stared at it.

Then handed it to me.

"Answer it," he said.

I swallowed hard and hit accept.

"Hello?"

The voice on the other end was calm. Smooth. Laced with a menace that didn't need volume to chill the bone.

"You made it farther than I expected, Nay."

Scar.

Just his name made my stomach tighten. His voice had that strange quality—half predator, half seducer. You could almost forget the blood he spilled because he spoke like he owned you before you even knew you were his.

"You sound winded," he continued. "Did Colt run you too hard tonight? Or was it the sniper rounds that got your heart pumping?"

I said nothing.

Scar chuckled.

"That silence of yours," he said. "It used to mean you were thinking. Now I wonder if it means you're starting to understand."

"Understand what?" I bit back.

"That I'm not chasing you," he said, voice softening in a way that made my skin crawl. "I'm *training* you."

I froze.

Colt stepped closer, jaw tense, eyes burning.

"You run. You bleed. You survive. But every time, you get a little smarter. A little harder. And I like my enemies sharp. What fun is it if you break too soon?"

"You think this is a game?" I asked.

He exhaled a slow, snake-like breath.

"No, love. This is a *sermon*. And the city is listening."

Something shifted then. A faint sound on the line—like paper being unfolded.

"You ever wonder how I found you tonight?" he asked.

My blood turned cold.

"Check the bag," Scar said.

The line went dead.

Colt moved instantly, dumping the duffel onto the floor. Among the gear, ammo, maps, and burner phones, was a folded sheet of paper. Bloodless. Crisp. Just lying there like it had always belonged.

I picked it up with gloved fingers.

On the paper: a single photo.

Me and Colt. On the rooftop earlier that night. We weren't looking at the camera. But Scar had caught the moment.

The *intimacy*.

The *closeness*.

My hand on Colt's chest. His lips almost touching my ear. The kind of picture you take when you're watching someone—not for hours, but *weeks*.

Scar had eyes we didn't know existed.

Eyes that *wanted* us to know.

Colt's jaw clenched. "He's not hunting us..."

I finished the thought. "He's circling."

For a long moment, we just sat there in the heat and dark. Listening to the silence between us.

Then I folded the picture back up.

"We end this," I said, voice low and raw. "Soon."

Colt nodded.

But something in his face said he was already expecting the cost.

And something in my chest said I might be willing to pay it.

Chapter 17 Fire for Fire

Bait doesn't have to be blood. Sometimes, it's memory.

The boiler room had gone quiet hours ago, but we hadn't moved. Not far, anyway. Just enough to find an abandoned back office tucked behind rusted pipes and broken conduit.

Colt had dragged in a splintered chair and flipped a battered crate into a makeshift table. The room was small. No windows. No exits but the one we'd come through.

We were trapped.

But we were also *focused.*

Nay sat across from me, her knees pulled to her chest, hair still damp from the rain. She was watching the flicker of candlelight dance along the cracked walls, but her mind—her mind was sharpening.

"I want him to feel what I felt when that picture hit my hand," she said softly. "Not fear. *Exposure.*"

Colt leaned forward, elbows on his knees. "So we flip it. We stop reacting and start pulling strings."

"How?"

He grabbed the burner phone off the crate and slid it toward her. "We build a trap."

Nay cracked her knuckles. "We need a location. Something Scar *can't resist.*"

"A name. A symbol. Something that makes him come out swinging," Colt agreed.

Her eyes narrowed, and then, like a blade drawn from velvet, her lips curled. "The boy he buried under that ferry pier. Malik."

Colt blinked.

"I pulled the name from the corner of one of those surveillance prints," she said. "Same timestamp. Scar's crew buried a body six months ago. Quiet. Off record. I think it mattered."

Colt leaned back, impressed. "You want to exhume a ghost."

She nodded. "Post a drop location online. Same alley. Same time. Fake vigil. But we don't go quiet. We tag it, leak it, whisper it to the right ears. We make him *think* someone's digging into the one sin he didn't want on record."

"And we wait?" Colt asked.

"No," Nay said. "We *watch*."

They started piecing it together. An anonymous burner message drafted for the right Telegram thread. A fake profile using a name close enough to a real street contact to feel legit. Even the wording felt like Scar's language—taunting, incomplete, *familiar*.

"Ask Scar about the pier. Ask him who Malik really was."

They planted it on message boards Scar's people monitored. Colt even forced a fake tip through a known dirty cop's burner, making sure the information bled into Scar's channels organically.

"He'll think it's one of his own," Colt muttered. "And that'll drive him mad."

Nay lit another tea candle with shaking fingers. The light caught the edge of her jaw, highlighting a bruise that hadn't faded yet.

"This isn't just about revenge anymore," she said. "This is about ending the ghost."

Colt nodded. "And maybe becoming a few ourselves."

Silence fell again.

But this time, it was the quiet of strategy. Of weapons being loaded, lines being drawn.

"We'll need eyes on the alley by 3 a.m.," Colt said.

Nay stood, slinging the duffel over her shoulder. "I'll go first."

Colt caught her wrist. Not hard. Just enough to hold.

"I won't let him touch you again."

Nay met his gaze, voice low and sure. "He already did. That's why I'm going to bury him."

The trap was set.

But bait, no matter how clever, always risked bleeding.

And Scar had a taste for both.

You can always feel it. When you're being watched. Even if you can't see who's watching.

The alley was darker than it should've been. Streetlights flickered but didn't hold. Windows overhead were all dark, like someone had warned the block to look away.

Nay stood at the edge of the shadows, her hood pulled low, hands buried in her coat pockets. Beside her, Colt crouched beside a trash bin, scanning rooftops, fire escapes, anything that might blink wrong or breathe at the wrong pace.

The fake vigil was already staged.

A single white candle burned at the base of a boarded-up brick wall, surrounded by a few hand-scrawled notes, a ragged photo of a boy no one would remember but everyone might believe in. *Malik.* Scar's buried past. A sin plucked from the muck and handed back to the streets.

A tag had been sprayed in red just behind it: "Ask Scar."

Nay lit another candle, placing it with calm, deliberate care.

"We stay twenty minutes," she murmured.

Colt checked his watch. "Eighteen left."

The tension wasn't loud.

It was *visceral.* Like a vibration behind your teeth. A crackling in the spine. Something *close.* Something *wrong.*

Colt's eyes scanned the windows again. "Top left. Movement."

Nay shifted her stance just slightly—cool, controlled. Her fingers ghosted toward her waistband where her knife sat snug against her ribs.

"No light behind it," he whispered. "Whoever's up there doesn't want to be seen."

"Good," she murmured. "Means he's watching."

Colt smirked grimly. "You always this calm when you're being hunted?"

"I was raised in shadows," she said. "You just learned how to fight in 'em."

He liked that. Even here, beneath flickering light and invisible rifles, she was calm. Focused.

At minute twelve, a wind kicked through the alley.

Not strong, but purposeful. Cold, like breath on the back of your neck. Colt noticed it too—his hand went to his waistband.

Then something shifted.

A car at the far end of the alley rolled forward two feet.

Then stopped.

No headlights. No engine rumble. Just… movement.

Nay stiffened. "That's not local traffic."

"Steel-belt tires," Colt muttered. "Too smooth for anything in this part of town."

Another candle blew out.

Nay didn't relight it.

"We're not alone," she whispered.

Colt gave a tight nod. "On my count, we fall back. Let the alley breathe."

She touched his wrist. "Wait."

A door cracked open at the far end.

Just a sliver. Just enough to show someone *was* there. A silhouette—broad shoulders. Stiff posture. Holding something long and black.

Not a gun. A camera.

They were being *recorded*.

Scar was watching his bait take form.

And he was *learning from it*.

They waited five more minutes. No gunfire. No voice in the dark. Just the cold, analytical gaze of someone absorbing the moment like a chess player watching the board reset.

Colt tapped Nay's back twice.

They slipped into the side alley without a sound.

Back at the safehouse, Nay didn't speak for ten full minutes.

Finally, she said, "He didn't take the bait."

"He studied it," Colt answered. "Which means he's not mad. Not yet."

She turned toward him. "Then we'll give him a reason to be."

Sometimes the fastest way to gut a lion is through its cub.

Back at the safehouse, the silence between them wasn't fear—it was calculation. Both were tracing the outline of the night in their minds: the camera. The ghost car. The door that opened, then shut like a threat.

Colt knelt in front of a half-broken desk, laying out what gear they had left—two burners, a scanner radio, a cracked police-grade tablet, and a thumb drive encrypted by someone Colt used to run ops with. Nay stood at the window, watching the street below without blinking.

"Scar watches us like we're amateurs," she said. "We need to show him we've got teeth."

"More than teeth," Colt muttered. "We need leverage."

She turned toward him. "Then we flip someone. Someone close."

The name came quickly.

Slink.

213

One of Scar's drivers. Twitchy. Small-time. He'd risen fast, too fast, riding on his cousin's name and Scar's good graces.

But Colt remembered him from a job two years ago—a botched cash drop in Koreatown that left Slink pissing himself in a motel bathtub.

"He's weak," Colt said. "Has a gambling issue. Last time I saw him, he owed money to two crews. If he's still alive, he's scared."

Nay grinned. "Then we make scared useful."

They staged the plan in layers.

First: Colt reached out through a burner text to a known number Slink used for his side deals. No name. Just a time and place. *You want out? Bring clean wheels. No trackers. Alone.*

Second: Nay flooded a private message board with a fake thread—an anonymous tip claiming **Slink had been seen talking to cops**. Just enough detail to be believable. Just enough sloppiness to seem real.

Third: They waited.

Slink showed up in a borrowed Civic, beads of sweat already dampening the collar of his oversized hoodie. He stepped into the abandoned bakery where Colt and Nay had taken cover, his eyes darting like he was expecting someone to jump out with a blade.

"You said you had something for me," he croaked.

Nay stepped forward, slow and deliberate. "We do. A way out."

"You working for the feds?"

Colt scoffed. "Does this look like a fed op to you?"

He gestured to the broken glass, the moldy bread racks, the hole in the ceiling where rain still dripped.

"We're the *only* chance you've got, Slink," Nay said, low and sharp. "Because we just made it *look* like you're flipping."

Slink paled. "What?"

Colt tossed a folded paper bag onto the table. Inside: a flash drive, two burner phones, and a fresh passport with Slink's name forged under a Ghanaian alias.

"You disappear now, Scar thinks you ran. You stay and he guts you. But if you *work* with us..."

"You live," Nay finished.

Slink blinked. Then again. His fingers twitched like he wanted to grab the passport and run but was still calculating what it meant to be caught holding it.

"What do you want me to do?" he asked finally.

Colt smiled. "Nothing yet. Just sit tight. Wait. We'll feed you lines. Fake intel. A few names. A few places."

"And when Scar starts to doubt his circle," Nay added, "he'll bleed it from the inside."

Slink left through the back door with the posture of a man walking into his own funeral.

But Nay watched him go like a chess piece she'd just sacrificed—and Colt knew better than to doubt her endgame.

"He's going to break," Colt said.

"Good," she replied. "I want Scar to hear it in his voice when he does."

By the time they returned to their base, Colt's burner lit up.

A message. No name.

Just three words:

"Slink's been flagged."

Scar had already noticed.

But they weren't scared.

They were ready.

Sometimes the loudest weapon is a whisper that hits the right ear.

Colt adjusted the earpiece, the static hum in his left ear giving way to the crackle of downtown interference. Nay sat beside him on the rooftop ledge, long legs crossed, her eyes locked on the intersection below like a sniper waiting on a pulse.

Rain slicked the city in chrome and shadow, the streetlights too dim to hide the tension rippling in the air.

"He's in position," Nay whispered.

"Copy that." Colt keyed the burner.

Slink's voice came through—thin, shaky, but clear. "Yo… they makin' moves on the Grandpoint stash. Said somethin' about a drop window tonight. Real talk, Scar… you might wanna check that yourself."

They waited.

No response.

Then, almost a full minute later—just when they thought the line was dead—Scar's voice came through like a blade:

"You better not be lying to me, little man."

Slink didn't respond. He didn't have to. The silence was its own confession.

Scar believed it.

Colt and Nay had fed Slink just enough half-truths to make the lie smell like truth. *Grandpoint* wasn't a stash house anymore—it was a condemned garage on the east end, rigged with two surveillance feeds and a kill-switch detonator Nay had programmed from scratch.

Their plan wasn't just to catch Scar moving.

It was to catch him *panicking.*

Because Scar, when calm, was lethal.

But Scar, when cornered?

Sloppy. Loud. Brutal.

Three SUVs rolled into Grandpoint fifteen minutes later.

Colt watched them from across the street, tucked inside an abandoned tax office with camera feeds running through a makeshift tablet dock. Nay sat behind him, a wire running from her laptop to the garage's fuse box.

On screen, Scar's men spread like a virus—searching the building, barking into radios, overturning crates that hadn't been touched in years.

"You sure he'll show?" Colt asked.

Nay didn't look up. "He won't send someone to clean up his own mess. He'll want to kill it himself."

"How poetic."

She smiled. "How predictable."

At 9:42 p.m., Scar arrived.

Not in a convoy. Not with fanfare.

He walked.

Black coat. Gloves. No umbrella.

Just a man with something to bury.

Colt straightened. "There he is."

Nay keyed the relay.

"Go wide," she said. "I want every step on record."

The trap was already closing.

Because once Scar stepped into the garage, a secondary burner Colt had planted in the backseat of one of the SUVs sent a silent ping—broadcasting a false location tag to a dirty cop Nay had on payroll, who owed her favors from another lifetime.

That cop? He'd already filed an anonymous report of gunfire at the same location.

Which meant within *ten minutes*, the **police** would arrive. The real kind.

And for once, Colt and Nay wouldn't need to pull the trigger.

"You realize what happens if he runs," Colt said.

Nay cocked her head. "He won't."

"You that sure?"

She turned to him, eyes unreadable. "Scar only runs when he has somewhere to go."

Sirens. Faint but building.

Colt checked the clock. 9:53.

Inside the garage, Scar barked orders. Someone slammed a metal crate. Another man hit a wall.

But Scar wasn't moving toward the exit.

He was digging.

"Shit," Colt muttered. "He's looking for bugs."

"Let him," Nay said calmly. "They're planted deep."

Colt gave her a side-glance. "If this works, it's not just Scar that falls."

She nodded. "No… it's his whole damn operation."

9:59. The first squad car rolled in fast, no siren, just lights. Two more followed.

Scar's men scattered like rats—but Scar stood still.

Inside the feed, his head tilted toward the blinking red light in the corner of the garage. He knew.

Colt watched him mouth something.

"Nay."

Colt's hands curled into fists.

Nay reached over and gripped them.

"Let him say my name," she whispered. "It'll be the last time he says it with power."

By the time the police burst into the garage, Scar was gone.

But not clean.

Colt hit play on the backup feed—a perfect, clear shot of Scar's face in full rage. Barking orders. Smashing crates. Holding a weapon he wasn't licensed to carry.

They'd gotten enough.

And now the streets would start to talk.

Scar's house wasn't just cracking.

It was *collapsing*.

Jahari Hasahi Malik

Chapter 18 Let the House Burn

The city always talks. You just have to know what silence means.

They sat on the rooftop of a defunct auto body shop, steam rising from coffee cups they hadn't touched, eyes fixed on the glowing billboard across the street.

WANTED: ARMED AND DANGEROUS. DOMINIC "SCAR" LEVY.

Scar's face glared from the digital screen like a brand falling from grace. A composite shot taken from the Grandpoint garage footage—angled just enough to show the gun in his hand, his snarl mid-command, and the chaos behind him.

Colt leaned back, sipping from the edge of his cup. "He's famous now."

"Infamous," Nay corrected. "There's a difference."

Below them, the city buzzed—more alive than it had been in weeks. Word was out. The king of the block wasn't untouchable anymore. Scar's lieutenants were either running or bleeding out.

Two stash houses had been hit by rivals overnight, and a third had been torched, likely by his own crew to destroy evidence.

Nay scrolled through her burner's feed. Screenshots of texts. Audio leaks. Surveillance shots.

Scar's empire wasn't just leaking—it was drowning.

And the sharks had begun to circle.

"This is where he gets dangerous," Colt murmured. "Cornered dogs don't bark. They bite."

Nay nodded, but her gaze was focused, distant.

"We've destabilized his control," she said. "Now we dismantle it."

"You think he'll come after Slink?"

"He won't need to. Slink won't last two more days on the street. That was the point."

Colt gave her a look. "You planned for that?"

She didn't blink. "He served his purpose. The next move has to hit Scar's ego."

"You mean his money."

"No," she said. "His myth."

They moved that afternoon.

No guns. No loud entrances.

Just a quiet, surgical strike to the one place Scar had never let anyone see from the outside: **The Haven**.

An upscale social club built in the bones of an old bank vault. It had survived gentrification, blood feuds, and city council bribes because it was

Scar's cathedral. He held court there—not in meetings, but with gestures, shadows, whispers.

If Grandpoint was a punch...

The Haven was the kill shot.

Inside, Colt flashed a forged access card. Nay wore a crisp black blazer over a body-hugging tank and jeans, hair pulled back, eyes sharp. They passed through the lobby, ignored the side-eyes, and walked like they belonged.

By the time the bouncer's radio crackled—
"Security alert, two unknowns on lower level"—

Nay had already slipped a burner behind the server's counter. A red light blinked beneath the mahogany. Recording. Uploading. Infecting.

The Haven's secrets would bleed online by nightfall.

Back on the street, Nay exhaled slowly.

Colt glanced over. "That felt... too easy."

"It was," she admitted. "Which means the next 24 hours won't be."

That night, **The Haven was trending.**

A blurred video leaked onto underground forums—Scar slapping a lower-ranking crew member, then tossing a bundle of cash at a woman who looked barely legal.

A second clip followed: footage of Scar's backroom, where illegal arms deals and off-books transactions played out like Netflix crime documentaries.

By morning, city officials had launched a "task force." Anonymous donors offered five-figure bounties for information.

Scar's silence had become his downfall.

He'd ruled by fear.

Now fear was turning *on him*.

On the rooftop, Colt lit a cigarette he didn't smoke.

"You ever think we'd make it this far?"

Nay didn't answer right away.

Then: "No. But I *damn sure* planned to."

The safehouse was different now.

It wasn't the stale, dusty hideout Colt had first brought her to. Nay had added something to it—an energy, a quietness that softened the edges of chaos.

A candle flickered near the boarded window.

Her boots were kicked off in the corner.

Colt's gun lay stripped down on the table, untouched.

They didn't speak at first.

The silence between them wasn't uncomfortable—it was earned.

Nay sat on the edge of the bed, fingers tracing the scar on her hip, the one she'd gotten climbing over broken glass on their second run.

Colt stood in the bathroom doorway, shirt half-unbuttoned, his gaze pinned to her like gravity.

"Do you miss it?" she asked suddenly.

He tilted his head. "Miss what?"

"Before all this. When it was just… survival. No stakes. No names."

He walked over, crouching in front of her. "Nah. I was sleepwalking then."

She met his eyes. "And now?"

"Now I'm wide awake. And every part of me hurts for it—but I'd rather bleed beside you than go numb again."

She touched his cheek, thumb brushing a faint bruise blooming beneath his eye.

"You always talk like the world is on fire," she murmured.

He smirked. "Maybe it is."

"Then burn with me."

Colt didn't kiss her at first.

He just leaned forward, resting his forehead against hers. The heat between them crackled, not wild, but deep. Heavy. Built from every escape, every bullet, every breath they hadn't had time to take.

When his lips finally met hers, it wasn't rushed—it was reverent.

Hands explored not just for desire, but for *memory*—the way her waist curved, the softness beneath the sharpness, the way her breath hitched when he dragged his thumb along her lower back.

Clothes peeled away like truths—one by one.

Her blazer slid off. His shirt crumpled between them. Her fingers curled into his spine as he lowered her to the mattress, every kiss a promise to come back alive. Every moan a confession with no language.

There was nothing hurried about them now.

Only heat. Trust. Hunger slowed into something sacred.

When they moved together, it was quiet. Intimate. Raw.

No walls between them.

No street names or aliases.

Just Colt and Nay—two people who had killed for each other, run for each other, survived everything except *this* kind of closeness.

After, they lay tangled in the sheets, sweat cooling against skin and moonlight casting them in silver.

Colt ran his hand down her spine. "You scare the hell outta me."

"Why?"

"Because if I lose you," he said quietly, "I lose the only real thing I've ever had."

She turned her face toward him. "Then don't lose me."

A long silence stretched between them.

Then Nay whispered, "What happens after Scar?"

Colt exhaled. "We burn the map. Start somewhere new. Write our own names."

She smiled softly.

"Then write mine in ink."

The knock came just after sunrise.

Three slow raps. Then silence.

Colt froze, halfway through buckling his jeans. Nay was still wrapped in the sheets, her body curling upright like instinct had gripped her spine.

"No one knows we're here," she whispered.

Colt grabbed his pistol from under the mattress.

The knock came again.

Two this time.

Then a pause.

Then one final tap—*sharp*.

Nay's voice dropped to a whisper. "That's not a knock. That's a signal."

Colt stepped to the door, glancing through the peephole.

A kid stood on the stoop. Couldn't have been more than ten. Skinny. Dirty hoodie. Red shoelaces that didn't match.

Colt opened the door just a crack.

"You Colt?" the kid asked.

Colt's jaw tensed. "Who wants to know?"

The boy didn't blink. He held up a burner phone, flipped it open, and pressed play on a voicemail.

Scar's voice crackled through:

"You keep runnin'. That's fine. I like the chase.

But you left ghosts behind, and I don't play fair.

Check your messages. I left you a gift."

The phone beeped.

Then a photo popped up on the screen.

It was *Marlene*—Colt's former handler. The one who'd gotten him fake IDs, safe routes, burner accounts. She was a ghost now. Retired. Hadn't been in the game in five years.

In the picture, she was duct-taped to a chair, blood dripping from her mouth. Her silver hair matted to her scalp.

 The background looked like a warehouse— gray brick walls, rusted pipes, a single flickering bulb overhead.

Colt's stomach dropped.

The caption underneath read:

"Shouldn't have trusted her.

Your past is my leverage."

Nay stepped beside him, jaw clenched.

"This is what he does," she said. "Takes hostages. Twists your guilt into chains."

Colt swallowed hard. "She got me out when no one else would. Hid me when I was burning everything down. She has nothing to do with this."

"He doesn't care. He's not hitting us with bullets anymore—he's hitting us with *memory*."

The phone beeped again.

A live feed now. Shaky video. Scar stood beside Marlene, knife in one hand, cigarette in the other.

"I warned you, Colt," he said, voice smooth and sharp as glass. "You brought her back into the game. That's on you."

Then, to Marlene, softly: "You raised a traitor."

Colt reached for the phone—but the feed cut to black.

"Where the hell was that filmed?" Nay asked, already pulling on jeans, boots, her pistol.

"I don't know," Colt muttered, eyes scanning the still frame burned into the screen. "But that pipe in the back—it's steam, not water. That's an old transit outpost."

"Sub-level?" Nay's eyes narrowed. "Under the garment district, maybe?"

Colt nodded. "Let's move."

Outside, the kid was gone.

In his place, a single red shoelace curled on the step—tied into a noose.

Scar had left his mark.

Again.

The warehouse reeked of mold, piss, and old electricity.

Nay stepped through the service entrance first, Glock drawn low, her boots silent against the concrete floor. Colt followed, his eyes sharp beneath the black hoodie pulled low over his brow.

Outside, dawn cracked faintly behind the soot-streaked windows, but inside—it was night. Always night.

No guards.

No screams.

Just the hum of fluorescent bulbs dangling from chains, flickering like a warning from a dying god.

"This the place?" Nay whispered.

Colt nodded. "Same pipework. Transit hub retrofit. This used to be where they stored derailed train engines."

"Perfect place to hide ghosts," she muttered.

They found the first body hanging near the old control booth.

A man, early 40s. Tattoos up both arms. Hands zip-tied behind his back, mouth gagged with a red bandana. The floor beneath him was smeared in blood, already darkened and sticky.

"Not Marlene," Colt said tightly. "Scar's message. He's clearing house."

"Or leaving one," Nay said, scanning the room.

A phone buzzed in Colt's jacket.

New message. No sender.

"Keep going."

They advanced.

A single hallway stretched beyond the loading dock—lined with rusted lockers, busted pallets, and graffiti like scars on the walls. One word kept repeating in red spray paint:

LIAR. LIAR. LIAR.

Then they heard it.

A *click*. Followed by the slow, mechanical *whirrrr* of an old security camera turning toward them.

"He's watching," Nay muttered. "Of course he is."

Colt stopped at a steel door at the far end. It had once been reinforced—now the hinges were blown out, warped from a blast.

He raised his gun.

Nay mirrored him.

Together, they stepped inside.

The room was cold. *Too* cold.

Blankets of plastic sheets lined the floor, and in the center—tied to a steel chair—was **Marlene**.

Alive.

Barely.

Her eye was swollen shut, lip split. Her fingers trembled as she tried to lift her head.

"Colt," she rasped. "You... son of a bitch... you brought hell with you."

Colt dropped his weapon and knelt. "I'm getting you out."

"You can't," she whispered. "He's not done."

Nay turned, scanning the shadows. "We need to move, now. There's a secondary exit—"

Her voice cut off.

A *beep* echoed in the silence.

Then a *whine*.

Beneath Marlene's chair, a blinking red light.

C4.

"Move!" Colt roared.

He grabbed Marlene, ripping the duct tape from her arms and dragging her across the plastic while Nay covered their exit. The timer ticked faster—ten, nine, eight—

They barely made it to the loading dock before the explosion ripped the back of the warehouse apart, the shockwave flinging them to the concrete.

Smoke. Dust. Alarms.

Colt rolled over, coughing. Marlene lay limp in his arms but breathing.

"Scar left her alive," Nay shouted, pulling him to his feet. "So he could make her *bait*."

Colt's face twisted in fury.

"That was a message," he said. "He's not running. He's *waiting*."

And somewhere—maybe two blocks away, maybe across the damn city—Scar watched the live feed cut to static.

He exhaled smoke from a black cigar, his knuckles still bandaged.

"Now we see what love does under pressure," he muttered.

And smiled.

231

Chapter 19 Hollow Echoes

The back of the van rattled like bones in a tin can.

Nay sat with her hand pressed against Marlene's side, trying to slow the bleeding. The bandages were makeshift—torn from Colt's shirt, wrapped tight—but they weren't enough.

Not for a woman who'd taken shrapnel to the ribs and kept breathing through it.

"She's fading," Nay said, her voice low but hard.

Colt didn't look away from the road. His jaw was clenched tight enough to crack teeth. Every turn of the wheel was a prayer. Every red light was a curse.

"Hold her steady," he muttered. "We're almost there."

They weren't going to a hospital.

Too risky.

Too traceable.

Instead, they were headed to a contact Nay hadn't seen in three years—an ex-trauma nurse named Sosa, who owed her a favor and lived above a boarded-up convenience store in East Bayview.

"You sure she's still clean?" Colt asked as they rounded the block.

"She better be," Nay said, eyes narrowing. "Or we all die."

Sosa opened the door with a shotgun in one hand and a cigarette in the other. Her afro was tied back with a silk scarf, and her eyes went wide when she saw the blood.

"Jesus," she hissed. "I told you I patch up bangers, not ghosts."

"She's both," Nay said. "And she saved us once. You owe me."

Sosa stepped aside. "Fine. But this makes us square."

The room was dim. Incense covered the scent of iodine and steel.

Colt laid Marlene out on a fold-up massage table. She groaned but didn't wake. Sosa moved like a surgeon—fast, efficient, cold. She didn't ask questions. Just cut, clamped, and stitched like the devil was coming through the floor.

Nay leaned against the kitchen sink, rinsing blood off her arms.

"She's stable—for now," Sosa finally said. "But if she moves too much or breathes wrong, it's over."

Colt stepped out onto the fire escape, needing air.

Nay followed him, the city glowing low beneath them like dying coals. Sirens somewhere distant. Helicopter shadows slicing through clouds.

"She's not gonna make it, is she?" Colt asked, voice raw.

"She might," Nay said. "If we finish this fast."

Colt didn't answer right away.

Then he pulled something from his pocket.

A USB stick. Black. Scar's insignia carved into one side like a mocking grin.

"Where'd you get that?" Nay asked.

"Found it on the floor next to the bomb rig," Colt said. "Scar wanted us to take it."

Nay's eyes narrowed. "Trap?"

"Maybe. But maybe it's also a way in."

They went inside, plugged it into an old burner laptop.

One file.

Video only.

Scar's face appeared—blood-streaked and calm, lit by the soft red glow of a warehouse camera. He looked directly at them, like he could see through the screen.

"If you're watching this, you lived. Again. But I promise you—it ends soon.

You want me? Come to the dock. Midnight. No guards. No traps.

Just you, and what's left of your soul."

He smiled.

"Let's finish the story."

The screen went black.

"Dock's a trap," Nay said.

Colt nodded. "So we set one of our own."

"Pressure don't create diamonds. It exposes fractures."

The laptop lid clicked shut with finality, but the silence that followed was louder than the video.

Colt sat on the edge of the couch, elbows on his knees, hands clenched so tight his knuckles looked like powdered glass. Across the room, Nay paced, every few steps pausing to glance at Marlene—still unconscious, still breathing.

"Midnight," Nay muttered. "We've got less than six hours."

Colt didn't answer.

She turned to face him. "Say something."

He looked up slowly. "What do you want me to say, Nay? That I'm ready? That I believe this ends at the dock? That I trust Scar to come alone?"

"No," she said, stepping closer. "I want you to say what you're feeling before we walk into hell again."

He stood. Too fast. Too sudden.

"I don't have time to feel. I've been surviving off muscle memory and fire since this started."

Nay stepped in, toe-to-toe with him now, her voice low but unflinching. "Bullshit. You feel everything. You just bury it under rage and bullets."

Colt stared at her, breathing hard. "And you don't?"

"I just stopped pretending it makes me weak."

That made something shift in him—small, but real. His shoulders dropped a fraction. His breath stilled.

"We can hit him," she said, softer now. "But not like this. He's baiting us emotionally. If we go charging in, we lose."

He nodded. "Then we do it cold. Sharp. You take the lead."

Her eyebrows raised. "You sure?"

Colt stepped closer. "You've always seen further than me. Even when I couldn't see past my own blood."

The space between them thinned—tension folding in on itself, not like a crash but like gravity pulling two planets closer.

Nay reached up and touched the side of his jaw. Rough stubble. A healing scar near his temple. Skin warm and damp from the stress.
"You're bleeding," she whispered.
"Doesn't hurt," he replied.
"Not the part I meant."

She kissed him then—slow, not soft.
It wasn't about lust this time.
It was war between their ribs. Surrender in the way their mouths met. A truce carved out of fire and ash.
Colt's hands slid under her shirt, calloused fingers dragging over old bruises and new heat. Her breath caught. The kiss deepened. Their shadows fused against the wall like twin scars refusing to fade.
When he pulled back, it was only far enough to rest his forehead against hers.
"If this is the end…"
"It's not," Nay said. "Not yet."

The plan came together in whispers and sharp breaths:
• Colt would circle around the dock through the shipyard, sniping Scar's men from a distance.
• Nay would go in as if she'd come alone—wearing a wire, using the drone to capture everything.

• If Scar got close, she'd keep him talking until Colt found the angle.

• No mercy. No second chances.

"We finish this," Colt said, voice hoarse.

Nay nodded. "And we bury the ashes."

Outside, thunder rolled somewhere off the bay.

The city held its breath.

So did they.

Together.

"The truth don't wait for the right time—it crashes through when it's ready."

Marlene stirred sometime after the plan was locked in.

The faint rustle of the bedsheet drew Nay's attention first. She turned from the window just in time to see the older woman's eyes blink open, glassy and unfocused, lashes damp with sweat.

"Marlene?" Nay was already at her side, crouched low, checking her pulse and bandage.

"Hey, hey… easy now."

Marlene winced. "Still alive? Shit."

"You're too damn mean to die."

A weak laugh fluttered from her lips. "Don't sweet-talk me, girl. Hurts to breathe."

Colt stepped into the room, looming in the doorway like a shadow stitched with fury and fear.

"You made it."

Marlene's gaze shifted to him. "Barely. But long enough to say something you need to hear."

Nay touched her arm gently. "What is it?"

Marlene licked her cracked lips. "Scar—he's not planning to end this at the dock. It's misdirection."

Colt's fists clenched. "You saw something?"

"No. Heard it. Before the blast, before you got there. One of his men slipped. Said something about 'the train lines.' Said it had to be ready 'for the girl.'"

Nay froze. "Me?"

Marlene nodded, grimacing as she tried to sit up. "He doesn't want you dead, Nay. He wants you taken. Wants to finish what he started—make you his message."

Colt's voice went cold. "No."

"I don't know what it means," Marlene rasped, "but the dock's a show. The real move is under the city."

The air changed in the room—sharp and sudden.

Colt turned away, pacing. "That bastard's pulling a double bluff."

Nay's eyes narrowed, jaw tight. "He's rerouting us. Luring us into a trap while he sets the real one up beneath."

Colt nodded. "The subway tunnels. He's got safe points down there. Old cartel hideouts. That's how he moves shipments unnoticed."

"And it's where he wants to cage me again," Nay said, voice like steel.

Marlene coughed, hard. Nay helped steady her with one arm.

"You listen to me," Marlene whispered. "I came back into this life for you. Don't let it eat you. Don't let *him* win."

Nay pressed a kiss to her forehead. "He won't."

Colt leaned against the wall, eyes narrowed in thought. "We change the plan."

"No," Nay said. "We evolve it."

They sat back down at the table, dragging new maps across the surface. Street routes. Sewer layouts. Transit schematics from Colt's old contacts in the city planning department.

"There," Nay pointed. "If he wants to vanish with me, he'll do it from this transfer hub— abandoned, but still wired. It leads straight to the docks."

Colt nodded. "We cut him off before he gets to either."

"How?"

"We bring the war underground."

Outside, the sky had darkened into a bruised purple, like a wound swelling in real time.

The clock ticked down.

The city waited.

And this time, Nay wasn't running.

She was hunting.

"Some wars end in blood. Ours ends in fire."

The rail yard was a graveyard of forgotten metal—old freight cars rusted to their spines, graffiti scrawled across their ribs like final prayers.

Colt parked two blocks out. They went the rest of the way on foot, gear strapped tight, every step pulsing with tension. Rain clung to their jackets. Sweat clung to their skin.

The entrance to the underground junction was hidden behind a slab of concrete that looked like a maintenance tunnel—unmarked, untouched by time. Colt found the latch first, pulling it open with a quiet groan of old hinges.

Nay slipped past him, Glock in hand, flashlight off. Only the faint glow of the city behind them lit their descent.

The steps wound down into the belly of the beast—slick stone, dripping pipes, and stale air that smelled like rot and rust.

"I count six men," Colt whispered, his eye to the scope of the rifle. "Two posted at the south platform. Two near the fuse box. One at the generator. One pacing the old platform."

"They expecting company?" Nay asked, crouching beside him behind an iron beam.

"No. Looks like they're securing gear, waiting on Scar."

"Then this is our window."

They split.

Colt moved left, down the narrow catwalk that ran along the track's edge. He disappeared into the shadow like he belonged there, a living ghost.

Nay slid along the opposite wall, low and lethal, steps silent between each rail tie. The vibration of the live line beneath her boots sent a familiar thrill up her spine—danger made physical, real.

She found the pacing guard first—lean, jittery, tapping the butt of his rifle against the wall like a nervous tic.

She didn't hesitate.

One step.

One press of the silencer.

He dropped before he could whisper regret.

Colt took down his first target with precision—a clean shot to the neck from behind a crate of ammunition. The body slumped sideways without a sound. He dragged it back into the shadows, breathing steady, every move practiced muscle memory.

Across the tracks, Nay dropped the next two in quick succession—one with a blade, the other with her gloved palm smothering a gasp before the pistol followed.

The last man near the generator tried to radio, but Colt intercepted him mid-transmission—ripping the wire from his collar before choking him out in a brutal, fast grip.

Silence returned.

They regrouped at the platform's edge—breathless but alive.

"That's all six," Colt whispered.

"No—Scar's coming," Nay said. "This was the staging area."

Colt nodded. "Then we need to turn this place into a coffin."

Together, they planted charges along the support columns and fuse box—repurposing Scar's own shipment crates for cover. Colt had wired C4 to a remote detonator he tucked into his boot, just in case.

They dragged two of the bodies into the center of the platform, posed like bait, rifles left intact and ammo spilled.

A message, written in Colt's sharp block handwriting, was tucked into one of their pockets:

"You taught us how to hunt. Now we're here to show you how we end it."

The trap was set.
The air felt like it knew.
Heavy.
Waiting.
Something ancient waking beneath the tracks.

Nay stood on the edge of the platform, Colt behind her, hand on her shoulder.

"You ready?" he asked.

She didn't answer right away.

Then she said:

"No more running. No more hiding. Let him come."

Chapter 20 One Clip Left

The Trap Springs

The docks were silent in that way only death could be—like the wind itself was holding its breath.

Scar stepped out of the matte black SUV, boots clicking against the weather-worn concrete of the Pier 17 warehouse district.

His eyes scanned the rows of shipping containers stacked like forgotten tombs, a grim smile curling on his lips. Something was off. Too quiet. Too still.

"Fan out," he ordered, voice low but sharp. His men obeyed without question, slipping into shadows with the efficiency of wolves hunting in formation.

Scar adjusted the grip on the gold-plated Beretta at his side. The same weapon he used the night he thought he buried Colt. The same one he'd use tonight to finish it right.

The whispers had led him here. A tip from a source who claimed Colt and Nay were using the docks to traffic intel, preparing to vanish.

Scar didn't believe in luck. But he believed in blood debt. And his shoulder still throbbed where Colt's bullet had kissed bone.

A gull screeched overhead, startled. Then… nothing.

He narrowed his eyes.

A single red dot danced across the nearest container. Then another. Then four more.

"Move!" Scar barked, too late.

The night exploded.

243

A cascade of flashbangs tore through the silence—white light, deafening sound, smoke curling thick and fast.

His men scrambled, some dropping. Others shouting into radios that went dead. The whole dock had been wired for chaos.

And in the blur of panic, through the rolling fog of smoke and light, Scar saw her—Nay—backlit against the orange flicker of the fire she'd lit herself. Rifle slung tight, eyes locked on him. Not a victim. Not prey. A hunter. Just like Colt.

Just like him.

Burn It All Down

Nay's pulse was steady, but her eyes were wild fire. Through the smoke, she tracked Scar's outline like a ghost—fluid, calculating. The night hissed with tension, lit only by flickers of fire catching on oil-slick puddles and the glint of broken glass.

Colt pressed up behind her, breath hot against her neck, rifle cradled in his arms. He didn't need to speak. She felt him—his calm, his rage, his need for this to end.

"He took the bait," Nay whispered, crouched behind a stack of crates. "We move on my mark."

Colt gave a single nod, eyes narrowed on the chaos they'd orchestrated. This wasn't revenge. It was reclamation. Every trap Scar had laid, they'd learned from. Every ambush, every burn, every betrayal—they'd turned it into strategy.

From their perch, they could see Scar's men panicking—disoriented, trying to regroup, their earpieces jammed by the tech Slink had wired into the surrounding towers. The disruption gave Nay and Colt precious minutes to press their advantage.

"We separate the soldiers from the snake," Colt murmured, pointing toward the north corridor.

"Scar'll head for the freighter. He always keeps his real business close to water."

Nay's eyes narrowed. "Then we gut it."

She tapped her comm twice, sending a low-frequency pulse that triggered a second wave of explosives—non-lethal this time.

 Smoke bombs burst along the perimeter, cutting off Scar's view and separating his guards from his path to retreat.

Screams echoed as Scar's men dropped behind cover, some firing blindly into the haze. Colt surged forward like a storm, knees pumping, rifle raised. Nay was just behind him, quiet but deadly, each breath synced to her steps. They moved like one body, one pulse.

Gunfire erupted to their left—short, controlled bursts. They ducked behind a forklift,

Colt ripping a flash charge from his vest and tossing it clean over the machinery.

Boom.

Light and silence again.

They burst from cover, moving fast, cutting through Scar's perimeter. Each target fell before they could react—shots placed with surgical precision. This wasn't a fight. It was a purge.

They reached the steel service door to the freighter's dock office. Scar's sanctuary. Colt pressed his back to it, listening. On the other side, silence—unnatural and heavy.

"He's in there," Nay whispered. "You feel it?"

Colt nodded. "Yeah. Like death waiting to be called by name."

She stepped closer, touched his jaw. "Then let's speak it together."

He kissed her hard—quick, brutal, desperate. Then she turned, rifle ready.

And they kicked the door in.

inside the Snake's Lair

The room was humid and pulsing with a stale kind of heat—the kind that clung to concrete and secrets. Scar's private office didn't look like much: walls of shipping manifests, faded nautical maps, and a single desk made of steel and blood money.

But Nay didn't need a trophy case to smell power. She felt it—the decay of someone who had lived too long in the shadows.

They moved in opposite directions, Colt sweeping left with his rifle drawn while Nay glided toward the rows of file cabinets bolted to the wall.

There was no sign of Scar yet, but his scent lingered—cheap cigars and cruelty.

Suddenly, movement.

A shot rang out from the catwalk above.

Colt dove, rolling behind a stack of overturned chairs as bullets carved through the air where he'd been seconds ago.

"Top level!" he shouted, snapping off three shots. A figure ducked out of view.

Nay was already in motion, climbing the side of the rusted shelving like it was a jungle gym. Her blade glinted in one hand, pistol in the other.

Colt flanked left, catching another guard in the hip with a clean burst. The man cried out and collapsed into crates.

Then a door slammed on the far side of the room.

Scar.

Colt didn't hesitate—he sprinted.

Nay leapt from the second-tier catwalk, landing with a solid thud and firing once mid-fall.

Her shot caught the last soldier in the throat, a gurgled scream choking out as he dropped.

She was already on Colt's heels.

Scar moved like a ghost through the next room, knocking over a rack of weapons as cover, then pulling the pin on a smoke grenade. It hit the ground with a **clang**, and soon they were swallowed by fog and noise. Sirens in the distance. Hissing radios. Echoes of boots hitting metal grates.

"Keep talking, Scar!" Nay growled, voice sharp in the smoke. "Ain't nowhere left for you to hide."

His voice came from everywhere. "Funny. I was just thinkin' the same thing about you."

Suddenly, Colt was tackled—Scar bursting through the haze like a devil from a war story, blade in one hand, pistol in the other.

They crashed into a table, both weapons clattering away. Colt caught a fist to the jaw, spun, and drove his elbow into Scar's ribs. They scrambled, traded blows like it was all they'd ever known.

Nay emerged from the fog, aiming to fire— only for Scar to shove Colt in front of her at the last second.

"Do it!" Scar barked, panting. "Shoot through him if you got the stones."

Colt spat blood, barely breathing. "Don't."

But Nay didn't hesitate. She fired low.

The bullet grazed Colt's thigh and slammed into Scar's side.

247

Jahari Hasahi Malik

Scar screamed, rage pure and animal.

Colt collapsed to his knees, hissing, but alive.

Scar staggered backward, clutching his side—
and fell through the rear door into the night.

Nay caught Colt before he dropped.

"You with me?" she asked, voice shaking,
hands covered in blood.

He grinned, teeth pink. "You shot me... sexy
as hell."

She laughed, tears brimming. "Don't die,
dummy."

"I'll die when you let me."

Outside, Scar was bleeding. Wounded.
Cornered.

But not gone.

Not yet.

The Last Echo

Colt leaned against the alley wall behind the
warehouse, his breathing ragged, thigh soaked with
blood. Nay crouched in front of him, hands shaking
as she tore open a bandage packet from her vest.

The air was thick with copper, smoke, and
silence.

"You're lucky that shot didn't shred your
femoral," she whispered, voice cracked.

Colt grunted, a grin twitching through pain.
"You looked too good in the fog. Couldn't even be
mad."

She smacked his shoulder—gently. "I shot
through you, Colt."

"And it was the most romantic thing anyone's
ever done for me."

They both laughed. Then fell silent.

Behind them, sirens wailed. Somewhere deeper in the city, Scar was bleeding and furious—and still alive.

"I should've ended it," Nay muttered, staring into the dark. "Right there. Put one in his head and walked away."

"But you didn't," Colt said. "Because you still think like someone who's trying to find a way out of this mess without becoming the monster."

She met his eyes. "Maybe that's the mistake."

"No." He touched her face, thumb brushing a smear of soot on her cheek. "That's the part of you I'd die to protect."

Nay leaned in and kissed him—slow, raw, and quiet. It wasn't lust this time. It wasn't heat. It was grief. Connection. The kind of kiss that needed no follow-up, because it said: *We lived. We bled. We're still here.*

They broke apart as headlights splashed across the alley wall.

A car screeched to a stop.

Slink stepped out, wide-eyed and panting. "We got a problem."

Nay rose. "Bigger than the one leaking on the sidewalk?"

He nodded. "Scar made calls. Deep ones. Word is, he ain't just local anymore. He's bringing people in. The kind that don't care about turf—they care about leverage."

Colt's jaw clenched. "You saying this isn't over?"

"I'm saying..." Slink looked between them. "You hit Scar hard. Humiliated him. His empire's shaking—but he's about to get desperate. That makes him unpredictable. And dangerous."

Nay's eyes narrowed. "Then we end it before he rebuilds."

Colt pulled himself to his feet with a wince. "We go to the source. Shut down every pipeline he has. Money, muscle, name."

Slink gave a cautious smile. "You ready for a war?"

Nay didn't flinch. "We already started it."

She took Colt's hand, their fingers interlacing like a battle flag unfurled.

Behind them, the warehouse still burned. A symbol of their defiance. A warning to Scar—and anyone else watching—that *Love Is a Loaded Clip*... and they had bullets left.

Epilogue

Three Weeks Later — New York City, Lower East Side

The rain hadn't let up in days.

It smeared the neon into watercolor nightmares across the windshield, and the rhythm of it drummed like a countdown on the roof of the black SUV idling at the curb.

Inside, Scar sat with his left arm in a sling, his right hand cradling a glass of whiskey that smelled like woodsmoke and vengeance. His face bore the fresh ghosts of healing cuts, but his eyes were alive—calculating, cold, and smiling beneath it all.

"They think they won," he said softly, to no one in particular.

Beside him, a new face—young, tatted fingers laced together, mouth pulled tight in silence. His name wasn't important. Not yet. But his loyalty had been proven in blood, and Scar had already begun calling him *Heir.*

A figure stepped into the back seat from the opposite door, soaked to the bone. She wore a long black coat and no expression.

Scar didn't look at her. "Is the contact confirmed?"

She nodded once. "Colt and Nay are in the wind. But not far. The girl from the warehouse—Marlene—she's on life support. They'll come back."

Scar swirled the glass. "Good. Let them."

He leaned forward, set the drink down on the seat, and spoke low.

"I don't want bodies this time. I want ghosts. Make them question who's alive. Who's safe. Who's next. Burn their world from the edges in. Slowly."

The woman didn't blink. "And the leak in your crew?"

"Plugged." He smiled, slow and sharp. "The next war isn't about muscle. It's about message. And mine?"

He finally turned, eyes alight with purpose.

"Mine's about to echo louder than gunfire."

The SUV pulled away, lost in the blur of city lights and rain.

www.ingramcontent.com/pod-product-compliance
Lightning Source LLC
Chambersburg PA
CBHW061426030726
47503CB00005B/1317